"Your head is filled with cotton candy," Matt said stubbornly

"And romantic drivel that belongs in fairy tales," he added for good measure.

"Attraction and love between two people isn't drivel," Willie exclaimed hotly.

"You're right. It's lust, pure and simple. Want me to show you?" he asked, stepping closer. With a smile that was pure devilment, he pulled her to him.

Willie barely had time to close her mouth before he covered it with his. She detected the tremor that rippled through him as they stood pressed together. She sensed the unexpected feeling in his kiss. Gasping for breath, she finally pushed at him.

"Hormones . . . right?" she asked, mischief in her eyes.

Matt looked at her, stunned. For once, he was speechless.

Pamela Roth, an established romance author as Pamela Toth, is an exciting new writer for Harlequin Temptation. Although she majored in the arts, Pamela says she never intended to become a writer until a few years ago, when she began reading romances by the dozen. She also loves to cook, even though she admits to sometimes forgetting dinner in the oven while in the throes of creation.

Pamela lives in western Washington with her husband, two teenage daughters and two Siamese cats.

Too Many Weddings
PAMELA ROTH

Harlequin Books

TORONTO • NEW YORK • LONDON
AMSTERDAM • PARIS • SYDNEY • HAMBURG
STOCKHOLM • ATHENS • TOKYO • MILAN

This books is dedicated
to the memory of Lynn Wicken,
sister-in-law and beloved friend.

Published June 1989

ISBN 0-373-25354-0

1

WILLIE WEBSTER had married a lot of people, but her next wedding was really special.

She dropped the lace curtain back into place and walked quickly to the parlor, green print caftan swirling around her petite figure. High-heeled shoes that added two inches to her five-foot-nothing tapped against the hardwood floor of the hallway. As she paused in the doorway, the parlor looked as it always did, slightly frayed around the edges.

Outside the small building, traffic rushed past on Aurora Avenue, one of Seattle's busy arterials. Willie's home, the Wishing Well Wedding Chapel, was bordered on one side by a car dealership and on the other by a combination minisupermarket and gas station.

Absently Willie patted her curly light red hair, then untangled the gold chains around her neck with impatient fingers. Matching bangle bracelets clinked together softly on her arm. Hearing a car door slam, she called to her Aunt Violet and turned toward the front entry.

As a knock sounded on the door, Willie reached for the knob and twisted it. A pale young woman with long, light brown hair stood before her, dark eyes filled with excitement. Willie hadn't seen Amanda Bailey for years, since Willie had been a camp counselor and the younger woman had been assigned to her cabin for the whole summer. Even though Amanda now towered over Willie, she was easy to recognize and quite pretty in a white dress and matching hat.

"Willie?" she said hesitantly.

"Amanda!" Willie opened her arms wide and the two friends embraced.

"I'd know you anywhere," they said in unison. Then, chuckling with delight, Willie stepped aside to let Amanda and the two people with her into the little pink house.

Willie's eyes widened as she noticed the big man standing behind Amanda. He was very attractive in a well-cut dark blue suit that hugged his broad shoulders, but he was much too old for Amanda, who was only eighteen. He stared down at Willie with a frown pulling at his dark brows.

"Mr. Peterson?" she asked.

The frown deepened.

Amanda giggled, making a tinkling sound, as Willie closed the purple door behind them. Then Amanda introduced him.

"This is my brother, Matt."

He enfolded Willie's outstretched hand in a firm grip, and she understood why he had frowned at her mistake. Amanda had alerted her on the phone that Matt was opposed to the wedding, and now Willie had mistaken him for the groom.

"You?" he asked, when Amanda gave him Willie's name. "You're the justice of the peace?"

"I am," Willie admitted with exaggerated patience. Because of her curly hair, the freckles that danced across her slightly upturned nose and her small size, she was used to reactions like his. Usually people expected a man to be doing her job, but Matt Bailey knew about Willie. Besides being Amanda's camp counselor the summer after the Baileys' parents had been killed, she and the younger woman had kept in touch by Christmas cards and the occasional letter ever since.

After greeting another young woman, who was to be Amanda's witness, Willie showed them into the parlor, where all of her on-site weddings were conducted.

Amanda seemed eager for Willie's approval. "Did you realize I'd get so tall?" she asked, twirling around for Willie's inspection.

"You've turned into a lovely young woman," Willie told her sincerely. "I knew you'd catch up to those long legs someday."

Amanda colored and smiled, flipping a curl over her shoulder. "I graduated with an A average," she said, glancing at her brother.

"I know. You told me in your last letter," Willie answered. "That's great."

"You should be going to college," Matt said, his voice husky.

He and his sister exchanged a long look and Willie was uncomfortably aware of the undercurrents flowing between them. As she searched for something to say to break the tension, Matt turned and went to the parlor window. It looked out over Aunt Violet's tiny herb garden.

Glancing up at the ornate grandfather clock, Willie asked, "Where's the groom and the other witness?"

"Craig should be here any minute," Amanda answered. "I hope nothing's happened to make him late."

"We should be so lucky," Matt Bailey growled over his shoulder, then turned his broad back to the rest of them.

Shocked, Willie looked from Amanda to her attendant, brows raised in silent inquiry. She'd been told of Matt's disapproval, but hadn't expected him to be so open about it.

"I'm sure that Craig's on his way," she said in soothing tones after Amanda made a face at her brother's back. Willie was just about to go and search for Aunt Violet, when the older lady appeared in the doorway, holding an ornate silver tea tray.

Aunt Violet wore one of the old-fashioned dresses she favored, with a lace collar and a cameo broach pinned at the front. Her thick hair was swept neatly into a knot on the top of her head, and wire-framed glasses hung around her neck on a chain. She would have looked much more conventional than Willie did in her caftan, except that Aunt Violet had a fondness for tinting her white hair. Usually it was light blue; today it was lavender to go with her dark purple dress.

Matt moved quickly to relieve her of the heavy tray, and Willie made the introductions. When her aunt faced Matt Bailey and took his hand after he'd set down the tea things, Willie was afraid the older woman was about the say something outrageous. Instead she merely winked at him and held on to his hand a moment longer than was necessary. Then she sat down regally by the coffee table and began to serve.

"You did want me to use the traditional wording?" Willie asked Amanda, speaking quietly as she sat next to her on the maroon davenport and patted her cold hand.

Amanda nodded and Willie wrote down her middle name and Craig Preston's full name in her book. Then she explained where everyone would stand and what to expect from the brief ceremony.

Ten minutes later there was still no sign of the groom. Willie approached Matt, who had returned to his silent vigil at the side window, ignoring the rest of them.

"Excuse me," she said in a low voice, "Craig's very late. If he doesn't get here soon, we'll have to postpone the ceremony. I have another party coming in shortly, and I'm booked for the rest of the day."

He turned to look down at her and Willie noticed again with a little shiver of response just how attractive he was. His face was strong and intelligent despite his remote expression, his coloring bolder than his sister's, even the brown eyes. Where Amanda's were warm and soft, his were narrowed and glittering, fringed with short, thick lashes below heavy brows. His hair was dark and neatly trimmed, and his skin was tanned, where Amanda's was pale.

Still, there was a family resemblance in their high cheekbones and wide foreheads, and they were both tall, though Matt was much more powerfully built than his slim sister. His appearance was compelling in an ungentle way. Willie would bet that the only civilized thing about Matt Bailey was his well-tailored clothes.

As he continued to stare down at her, she tried out a tentative smile, wondering what it would take to crack his forbidding expression. His lips remained a grim line as his steady gaze swept the length of her.

"I'm opposed to this marriage," he said finally to Willie, who was beginning to feel uncomfortable under his scrutiny. "Amanda's fresh out of high school and they're both too young to know what they want." His wide chest rose and fell on a deep sigh. "I never thought my little sister would end up getting hitched to a bum like Preston by a redheaded leprechaun who tells fortunes on the side."

"It's my Aunt Violet who reads palms," Willie answered coolly. "And you're mixing your metaphors. Leprechauns grant wishes. It's usually Gypsies who do fortunes. But tell me," she continued, easing into the insult smoothly, "how did a nice girl like Amanda get saddled with a stuffed shirt like you for a brother?"

Something flashed in the dark eyes that watched her, something quite different from their usual chilly remoteness. Surprised at the dart of satisfaction she felt in drawing a response from him, Willie retreated without giving him a chance to reply.

Amanda was sitting with her friend Melodie, and the prospective bride bore all the outward signs of a woman in love. Willie could recognize them easily; she'd been marrying couples for over four years. Some people might think it a strange way to use a law degree, but it gave her tremendous satisfaction. Some of her marriages kept in touch, sending her cards every Christmas, and one particular couple sent her a box of chocolates on Valentine's Day. Her work was much more fulfilling to her than working in a lawyer's office had ever been.

Despite Willie's question and the way she'd stepped away from him, Matt found himself watching her with reluctant fascination. She wasn't at all what he'd expected. He sensed a temper and spirit beneath the freckled skin and jingling gold jewelry, and he wondered how her body was shaped under the green tent that hid it. He'd breathed in the scent of something spicy before she'd swirled away, and the intriguing fragrance still lingered.

Willie's fingers tugged at the small hoop in her ear, and Matt realized with a start of surprise that the lobe was pierced in three places. Two diamond studs winked at him through her light red curls. He moved closer, touching her arm. Then his hand fell away when she eyed it balefully.

"I could show you what kind of a stuffed shirt I am," he felt compelled to whisper into that dainty pink ear. "You may be pleasantly surprised." The words startled him almost as much as they obviously did Willie; it was out of character for him to blurt something without thinking it over first.

Willie managed to totally ignore his last remark, though she silently acknowledged the challenge of his veiled threat. Perhaps she had unwittingly asked for it; she herself had been uncharacteristically rude.

"Shame on you," she couldn't help but scold, eyes widened and voice quivering with righteous indignation. "You should be supporting your sister, not trying to undermine her confidence. Amanda may be young, but she knows what she wants and she's madly in love."

Bailey flushed a dull red at her words. Obviously he wasn't used to being criticized.

"I had a feeling that madness entered into it somewhere," he drawled. "But I'm here, aren't I? Under the circumstances, I think that's support enough. And don't bore me with any romantic notions of love conquering all." He returned Willie's disapproving stare.

Despite the disturbing undercurrents flowing between them, she didn't try to mask her dislike and neither did he. Amanda's letters had contained countless complaints of his heavy-handed attempts at raising her alone, and Willie was surprised he hadn't found some way to put his sister in a convent. Perhaps he'd tried.

Unable to think of a suitable reply, she excused herself and swept over to where the bride-to-be was sitting and twisting a delicate lace handkerchief into a tortured mess. The clock had chimed the quarter hour some minutes before, and Willie, too, was getting concerned.

"Craig's almost half an hour late," Amanda said, eyes swimming with unshed tears. "Something awful must have happened."

Willie tried her best to reassure the younger woman, then consulted a large appointment book. "Perhaps he's had a flat tire," she said, looking for the right page. "We still have a few minutes. Then I'll be all through at seven tonight, and I can marry you anytime after that." She glanced up at Amanda's brother with exasperation when he stopped in front of them. He was the one who should be comforting his sister, not Willie.

"Come on, Mandy," he said, jamming his big hands into the pockets of his slacks.

Willie did her best to ignore how his impatient movement had strained the material across tantalizingly muscular thighs. Her efforts were only partially successful.

"Admit that you made a mistake, and let's go home," he said roughly. "Preston's not going to show. I always knew he was a coward as well as a wimp."

Willie's mouth dropped open at his heartless words, and Amanda jumped up from the couch. She was almost as tall as he was, and they stood nose to nose, brown eyes blazing. "Don't you talk about Craig like that," she said, chin jutting. "I love him and he'll be here."

Willie resisted the urge to applaud her show of spirit, but just barely.

"Now, Mandy—"

"He must be lying somewhere badly hurt," she wailed, starting to cry in earnest. "I just know it."

Willie watched Matt hesitate, then raise his hands to comfort her. Things were rapidly falling apart. Amanda twisted away, and after glancing at her attendant, who sat looking helpless, Willie stood and put a supportive arm around the sobbing bride. It wasn't easy. Amanda was a good eight inches taller than Willie in spite of the high heels.

Matt took Amanda's hand and attempted to pull her away. Glaring up at him, Willie tightened her arm. Amanda was doing her best to cry on Willie's shoulder, despite the height difference.

Matt's lips thinned as irritation prickled through him, and he dropped Amanda's hand, only to take her elbow, instead. He'd been opposed to this wedding from the start, and it gave him no satisfaction that he'd been right about Preston. He wished he had his hands around the young punk's neck right now. Looking past his sister, whose sobs had grown quieter, Matt's gaze collided with Willie's.

What an odd name for such a fragile and pretty woman. Hardening his heart, he ignored the pleading expression in her wide gray-green eyes. Obviously her head was stuffed too full of romantic drivel for her to see that Amanda was making a terrible mistake.

"Let's all sit down and have some more tea," Aunt Violet exclaimed cheerfully. "There may be a message about your young man's whereabouts in the leaves," she told Amanda.

Willie groaned silently and rolled her eyes, hoping that Aunt Violet wouldn't get started on that.

Determined to distract her, Willie waited until they were all seated, then turned to Matt. "Amanda told me you're a lawyer," she said. "Corporate or criminal?"

The grin that lifted the corners of his wide mouth made Willie feel as if she'd just stepped into quicksand. Before she could examine the strange sensation, he answered her casual question.

"I specialize in divorces," he said, watching her closely. "Also palimony suits, custody settlements and prenuptial agreements."

"Oh, I see." Willie was sorry she'd brought the subject up. No wonder the man seemed so cynical about marriage.

"In other words," he continued with apparent relish, "I finish what people like you start. I've already offered my sister free legal representation when she needs it," he added, his voice unbearably smug. "Kind of a wedding present."

Willie ground her teeth and tried to think of a suitably squelching reply. Amanda buried her face in her hands, beginning to cry again.

"Now see what you've done," Willie snapped at him.

Matt blinked in surprise. "What *I've* done?" he echoed.

"Yes," Willie said, taking a quick breath before continuing. "I've told her I can marry them this evening. If you'd quit trying so hard to upset her, I'm sure Amanda would realize that her fiancé has only been delayed. Or perhaps he's gotten lost. He did tell me on the telephone that he's from out of town."

"Yes," Matt said with scorn in his voice. "He's in the navy, barely twenty-one years old. Amanda met him at the library where she works."

"How romantic to marry a member of our armed forces who's defending our country," Willie exclaimed, patting Amanda's hand. Her fingers touched the soggy handkerchief and she quickly withdrew them.

Matt snorted derisively. "He's a cook," he said.

As Willie was about to suggest that they return home and wait for Craig to get in touch, the doorbell pealed several times in rapid succession.

Aunt Violet sailed from the room to answer it, lavender bun quivering. A moment later a thin, highly agitated young man in uniform burst into the parlor, carrying a corsage in a plastic florist's box. When Amanda saw him, she launched herself into his arms with an enthusiastic whoop. Another sailor appeared behind them.

Matt's expression turned glowering and Willie noticed that his big hands had closed into white-knuckled fists at his sides. Aware of impending disaster and the arrival of another wedding party out front, Willie stepped between Matt and Craig, who was kissing Amanda with great vigor.

"Am I too late?" he asked anxiously, coming up for air but retaining a tight hold on his now glowing bride-to-be.

Ignoring Matt's muttered comment and Amanda's questions, Willie smiled sympathetically. "I'm afraid so," she explained gently. "I have another group scheduled." As if on cue, the doorbell rang again.

Aunt Violet rushed out.

"I've already explained to Amanda that I'll be happy to marry you when I finish here at seven. Will that be convenient for all of you?"

"There's a problem," Craig said quietly. "I can't find the license. That's why I was late."

Willie stared at him in dismay. "I can't marry you without it. Have you looked everywhere?"

He nodded. "I swear I got one. Couldn't we—"

Willie shook her head reluctantly. "We have to have a license."

Amanda looked as if she were going to break into fresh tears. To Willie's surprise, Matt moved over and put a comforting hand on her shoulder.

"The courthouse is closed tomorrow," Willie said. "You won't be able to get things straightened out until Monday. I promise to fit you in after that, no matter what."

"But I've only got a weekend pass," Craig said. "I have to be back on the base Monday morning."

"Oh, dear," Willie said with a sigh, wondering what to do. She couldn't marry them without a license; it wouldn't be legal. "Can you explain things to your commanding officer? Perhaps he'd understand?"

Craig released Amanda and smacked his fist into his other hand. "If only I hadn't lost it," he said. "I'm sorry, honey."

Amanda's attention was instantly diverted from her own disappointment as she tried to reassure him.

Only Matt didn't look upset as he stood silently by. Perhaps he was right and they were too young. Still,

Willie hated to see Amanda so sad. It reminded her of all the tears a much younger Amanda had shed that summer long ago. At nine years old it had been very difficult for her to understand why God had allowed her parents to be killed suddenly, leaving her to be raised by her elder brother. It had taken much time and patience on Willie's part to help Amanda through that difficult summer, and now the tears brought it all back to Willie.

Craig's friend spoke up. "The old man may go for it and give you another pass," he said, clapping Craig on the shoulder. "Remember what he did for Crackowski when his mother fell and broke her hip."

Craig sighed and raked a hand through his short hair. "Yeah," he said. "It's a shot, anyway."

He smiled shakily at Willie. "We'll call you," he said. "Meanwhile Amanda and I have some talking to do. Come on, hon," he coaxed, taking her hand.

Matt stepped squarely in front of the young couple. "I'll see you at home tonight," he told Amanda.

His voice was firm and Willie knew there was a message in it. No honeymoon before the wedding.

Amanda glared at him for a long moment. It was Craig who finally broke the uneasy silence.

"I'll bring her home after we have some dinner, sir," he said. "Since we're all dressed up, I'm taking Amanda someplace nice. We'll drop Melodie off."

Matt nodded and stepped aside. Apparently Craig's answer had satisfied him. Willie breathed a sigh of relief. The other party was still milling about on the small front porch.

IT WAS SEVEN-THIRTY that evening when Willie finally had a chance to slip into worn jeans and a T-shirt and put her feet up. Aunt Violet had gone to evening services, and Willie had the small house to herself. She sighed and stared at the fuzzy blue slippers on her aching feet. Not for the first time did she wish she were taller so she wouldn't have to wear such high heels for work.

She was thumbing through the TV guide, when there was a knock on the door. Glancing out the window to make sure the neon sign was off, she shuffled to the entry. The knock sounded again, its aggressive pounding reminding her of Matt Bailey. She flipped on the porch light and opened the purple door.

Matt had just lifted his hand to knock a third time, when the brightly painted panel swung inward. He had to blink twice before recognizing the pixie who stood there as the same woman he'd met earlier. She'd looked young in the colorful caftan; in denims and a pink T-shirt that clashed alarmingly with her orange hair she could have passed for a teenage baby-sitter.

"Come in," Willie said, surprised to find him on her doorstep. He'd changed his clothes, too. Instead of the dark suit he'd had on earlier, he wore a plaid shirt under an open suede skin vest and snug tan jeans above brown Western boots. He still looked powerful and attractive, but now he looked powerful, attractive and human. Willie followed him as he headed straight for the parlor, not bothering to return her greeting.

"Come into the living room," she said. "We save the parlor for weddings and palm readings. You don't strike me as looking either to get hitched or to have your fortune told."

She could see the backs of his ears redden before he turned around. "You're right," he said in a deep voice. "I want you to use your influence on Amanda and talk her out of this crazy marriage idea."

His words made Willie stiffen. "I don't think it's a crazy idea," she said. "It's clear to me that Amanda and Craig love each other very much. Perhaps it's time you stopped interfering in her life."

Anger darkened Matt's features. "How can you condone this wedding? Amanda's only eighteen. She should be going to college in the fall. Are you so hungry for a fee that you don't care how much damage you do?"

Willie was appalled at his accusation and her fingers itched to slap his face. "I think you'd better leave," she said, whirling toward the front door.

Before she could take two steps, he grabbed her arm.

"You shouldn't have done that," Willie muttered, totally out of patience with his overbearing manner.

In less than the blink of an eye, Matt found himself sprawled flat on his back in the middle of the faded Oriental carpet. For a moment he just lay there, too stunned to move. Then he gingerly wiggled his fingers and moved one foot, checking for damage. Eyeing her warily, he sat up.

"How'd you do that?" he asked, voice incredulous. God, she was a foot shorter than he was and easily eighty pounds lighter. Her cheeks were still flushed with temper, but there was an expression of shock on her face that surprised him. She stretched out a hand and Matt automatically jerked back.

Willie managed a smile and put her curled fists onto her slim hips. "Going to sit there all night?" she taunted.

Matt could feel a hot blush of color run up his neck and across his tight face. He got to his feet with an uncharacteristic lack of grace.

"I have to apologize," she said, her smile replaced by a more earnest expression. "I overreacted."

For a moment he looked at Willie as if he would like nothing better than to strangle her, then leery admiration tugged the corners of his mouth into a reluctant grin. "Apology accepted," he said.

Willie let out a sigh of relief. She'd reacted on pure instinct and was now appalled at what she'd done. There seemed to be no middle ground with Matthew Bailey; she either wanted to feast her eyes on his virile good looks, or kill him. But Matt was a lawyer. What if he sued her? The thought was a sobering one.

"Thank you," she said.

Willie led the way into a shabby but clean living room. Matt followed, watching with interest the way her hips swayed as she walked and the curve of her behind in the tight jeans. He decided that she didn't look like a teenager, after all.

"You made a nasty slur against my integrity," she reminded him, deciding to take an offensive stand as she indicated a worn blue chair. "Why don't you sit down and explain to me why you're so opposed to Amanda's wedding?"

Matt sat warily, never taking his eyes off her. He still couldn't figure out how she'd thrown him so effortlessly. She'd really caught him with his pants down, but it wasn't going to happen again. Not unless it was his idea, he amended, eyeing the way she filled out the snug shirt. With difficulty he brought his attention back to why he was there.

After Matt had rambled on for several minutes about raising Amanda ever since their parents had died, repeating what he'd said earlier about her being too young, Willie shook her head vehemently.

Matt's voice faltered to a stop.

"I'm terribly sorry about your parents," Willie began thoughtfully, "and I know that Amanda's young, but in the eyes of the law she's old enough to get married without your consent. You don't have any right to stop them, and if you insist on clinging to this inflexible attitude, you'll lose her for good." She was about to add that she would talk to Amanda herself, when he spoke again.

"She's ruining her life," he repeated stubbornly.

"But it is *her* life, and you have to allow her to make her own mistakes."

Matt's jaw hardened. "I know what's best for my little sister," he insisted.

"This is getting us nowhere," Willie said, rising. They both needed to calm down. "Would you like a cup of tea?"

When he nodded, she continued in a conversational tone, "Aunt Violet has used the mint leaves from her garden in a new blend I've been meaning to try. It'll only take a moment." Perhaps Matt would use the time to do some thinking. Willie could see that his authoritarian attitude would only bring disaster.

She was back moments later with the tea tray. Matt, who'd taken off his suede vest before he sat down, looked on as she poured the steaming green liquid. Cautiously he took a sip.

"It's very good," he said, somewhat surprised.

"I take it you're not usually a tea drinker?"

"No, coffee. Gallons of black coffee, especially when I'm working."

"You should switch to decaffeinated," Willie remarked.

"Caffeine's why I drink it."

"Oh." She sipped from her own cup, not sure what to say next.

"You're probably right, though," Matt agreed, setting the delicate porcelain cup down on its matching saucer.

He leaned forward, his loosely joined hands dangling between his knees. His head was bowed. Willie couldn't help noticing the way his dark hair gleamed richly in the soft glow of the lamp.

"I don't know what to do," he confessed after a long moment of silence broken only by the ticking of the old clock. His broad shoulders drooped dejectedly. "I love Amanda very much."

His admission surprised Willie. Not the fact that he loved Amanda; she had assumed that all along. But Matt didn't strike her as a man who shared his feelings easily, and the confusion in his voice reached out to her as little else would have. She felt herself softening toward him.

"You're not married," she said, wishing there were someone who could share his dilemma and his pain.

"Divorced."

"I'm sorry." She remembered from Amanda's Christmas cards that he had been married briefly. It hadn't lasted and Amanda had been delighted when it had ended.

Absently Matt took another swallow of tea, which by now had cooled slightly. "Don't be sorry. It was a long time ago and the whole thing was a mistake from the beginning. Amanda and Michelle disliked each other on sight and never learned to get along."

He was silent for a moment and Willie realized how difficult it must have been for the newlyweds to cope with an insecure preteen who had probably thought her place in her brother's heart was being usurped.

"What about you? Have you ever been married?"

Willie shook her head and smiled, her dreamy gaze focusing on something beyond Matt's shoulder. "When I marry, it will be for life," she said with total self-assurance.

"Who's the lucky guy?"

"Oh, I haven't met him yet," Willie said. "But I'll know when I do."

"Love at first sight?" Matt's tone was scornful.

"I don't know about that," Willie said. "But the minute I meet him, I'll know that he's special."

Matt ran his fingers through his hair, barely able to prevent himself from rolling his eyes. There wasn't much point in trying to reason with a certifiable hearts-and-flowers romantic. Real life would disillusion her soon enough.

He studied Willie's smile and the light in her eyes. For a moment he felt a twinge of regret that someday that light would dim, her smile would become less open, more guarded. He wondered why it hadn't happened yet.

"Good luck," he said dryly.

"Thank you."

He looked closer, but apparently she'd taken his words at face value. Once his vision had been almost as rosy as hers, but his parents' unhappy marriage followed by one of his own, plus the daily handling of other couples' divorces had cured him of all that. He sighed deeply, thinking he might as well leave.

"You're not losing her, Matt," Willie said, misinterpreting his sigh. Trying to comfort him, she patted his arm.

Matt stared down at her small hand with its short oval nails before covering it with his own. When his gaze met Willie's she realized how close they'd somehow come to be. She could see flecks of light in the eyes she'd thought were almost black.

Her fingers were tingling strangely under his warm skin, and she could see the way his nostrils flared when he breathed. Her brain sent out a message to her fingers to pull away from him, a message her fingers blatantly ignored. Her own breath was trapped somewhere between her lungs and her throat.

Not taking his eyes off the woman next to him, Matt stood, pulling her up with him. She didn't resist. His hands slid to her waist as a tiny moan rose from her throat. It fired his blood and strengthened the curiosity that had been building since that afternoon. Curiosity about the taste and texture of her soft mouth.

Willie's spicy scent rose around him as she tossed her head. Her gray-green eyes had widened when his hands had encircled her narrow waist, but her eyes held no fear or nervousness. The want that had smoldered below his consciousness struggled to burst forth, but he refused to submerge his common sense in the river of desire he could feel rising within him.

Willie's palms lay against Matt's chest as if she wasn't sure whether she wanted to push him away or hold him close. While she was trying to choose, Matt made the decision for her, giving in to the desire that coursed in his blood.

He lowered his head, but Willie seemed to snap out of the spell that had been weaving itself around both of them, and she stiffened in his arms. An image of himself lying flat on the carpet as she stood over him, dusting off her hands, danced before his eyes, quelling his ardor. The expression on her face had closed, becoming unreadable, and Matt wasn't foolish enough to risk another blow to his pride, not to mention the various easily bruised parts of his person. Reluctantly he straightened.

"Willie . . . ?" he questioned as the front door burst open.

"Willie," echoed Aunt Violet, "who's there? There's a strange car parked out front."

Matt dropped his arms away completely and stepped back, muttering a word that made Willie's eyes widen. She moved away from him quickly, unable to meet his gaze. She was scarcely able to believe she'd almost been caught necking with a divorce lawyer. Somehow that would be worse than almost anyone else she could think of, except perhaps a Catholic priest.

Aunt Violet hung up her coat and entered the living room. Greeting Matt with a searching stare, she settled into her favorite willow rocking chair. "Would you like me to read your palm?" she offered. "I have a feeling your future would surprise you."

"No, thanks. I just dropped by to discuss my sister's wedding with Willie."

"Doesn't seem to me there'd be anything to discuss," Aunt Violet said with a little sniff. "It's *your* future that's going to be interesting."

"That's enough, dear," Willie cut in, knowing how persistent her aunt could be. The older lady was dying to see the lines on Matt's hand, and some deep-seated instinct made Willie do her best to distract her. "Matt undoubtedly has enough on his mind. Besides, he was just leaving."

"I was?"

Willie thrust Matt's suede vest at him, and his big hands closed around it automatically as his dark brows rose.

"Yes," she mouthed, her back to her aunt, whose curiosity Willie could almost feel. She would have to have a talk with Amanda before she said anything more to Matt. Willie still didn't think he was right to try to make Amanda and Craig wait, but it couldn't hurt to check things out herself. "I'll see you when the ceremony is rescheduled," she told him at the door. "Please don't try to screw anything up."

His grin was rueful. "Preston can manage that all on his own," he said, staring at her tempting mouth. She was cute, and responsive, but definitely not his type. He would have to remember that.

"We haven't finished discussing the situation," he said. "You're making a mistake if you think I've given up."

His strong chin was tensed with determination and his dark eyes were narrowed. Willie had the sudden thought that he would be a devastating adversary but a powerful friend.

"Good night," she said quickly as he stepped onto the porch. Before he could reply she shut the door, then leaned against it with a sigh of relief. Her heart was tripping in double time and she tried to tell herself it was only because she was concerned for Amanda.

"Willie, why don't you let me see your palm?" Aunt Violet called from the living room. "It might be pretty interesting."

Willie pictured Matt's dark eyes and the firm curve of his mouth, and her fingers curled protectively into fists. No way, she thought. Aunt Violet's knowing looks and satisfied chuckles were the last thing she needed.

2

TUESDAY MORNING Willie was gathering up everything she needed to perform an outdoor wedding ceremony when the doorbell rang. Glancing at her watch, she muttered under her breath and answered the summons. If she didn't hurry, she'd be late for her appointment.

Matt Bailey stood there, resplendent in a pearl gray three-piece suit and what Willie guessed was an Italian silk tie. Her startled gaze swept the length of him, down to his shiny black dress shoes and back up to his clean shaved face.

"What are you doing here?" she asked ungraciously. "I'm late for a wedding."

"I need to talk to you," he replied, eyeing her casual clothes doubtfully. "You don't look like a J.P. on her way to work to me."

"Take my word for it," she said. "I'm running late." Suddenly inspiration struck. "If you want to talk, you'll have to ride along." She picked up her purse and nylon duffel bag as she pushed past him, locking the door behind her after he meekly followed.

Matt had no choice but to climb into the passenger side of her ancient Corvair or be left in its dust. How long could this wedding of hers take? He had an appointment in two hours with Lee Timball, a wealthy client who seemed to make regular use of Matt's services. Timball's last divorce had cost him plenty. Still, the man had refused a prenuptial agreement for wedding number four and now here he was, paying through the nose to a greedy little opportunist who'd never have to work again.

Matt had been deep in thought until he noticed they were turning onto the approach for the Evergreen Point Floating Bridge. What kind of wedding were they going to, with Willie dressed the way she was, in faded jeans and a fuchsia polo shirt that should have clashed with her hair but didn't? He looked skeptically at the running shoes on her small feet as she shifted and accelerated onto the wide, flat bridge that floated on a series of pontoons.

"Where are we going?" he finally asked.

"Issaquah."

Willie considered herself fairly worldly despite having been raised by a widowed minister, but the curse Matt muttered brought fresh color to her cheeks. "You're lucky it's illegal to stop on the bridge," she told him. "Or I'd put you out right now."

Startled, Matt apologized. "What kind of ceremony are you going to perform dressed like that?" he asked, thinking of the appointment it appeared he was going to miss.

"Wait and see," Willie told him, trying to suppress a grin. She would be willing to bet that Matt had never attended a wedding quite like the one they were going to. It seemed to her that his composure needed a little shaking up, and maybe she was just the person to do it.

"I wish you had a car phone," he grumbled, glancing at his thin gold watch.

Willie made no reply, humming instead to the music on the radio as she concentrated on the heavy traffic. Matt decided to save what he wanted to discuss with her for the ride back to the wedding chapel. That would give him a chance to prepare his arguments, make sure he presented them in the best possible light. It was a habit that had contributed to his success as a lawyer and he made good use of it as they exited the bridge and sped down Interstate 90.

Neither spoke again until Willie pulled into the parking lot of a small airport. Matt turned to her, full of questions as she shut off the motor and unsnapped her seat belt.

"No time to talk," she said before he could even open his mouth. "Follow me."

"I need to phone my office," he said as she began to walk across the grass toward a small knot of people standing in front of a twin engine plane.

"Later," she replied, then asked one of the foursome if the group was the Ingalls party. When the young man nodded, she introduced herself, then turned to Matt, who was studying the aircraft with a wary expression.

Matt eyed the plane's faded paint with a distinct lack of confidence. He flew on commercial airlines fairly often, but had never quite gotten over the idea that the sky was meant for birds, not machines. It was probably too much to hope that the wedding ceremony was going to take place somewhere on the ground.

"Where's your other witness?" Willie asked one of the men, just as Matt was about to suggest that he find a phone booth, then wait for her at the car.

"He hasn't shown."

Willie glanced at the pendant watch that hung around her neck. "We have to go up now," she said, "or you won't be through here in time to make your flight from Sea-Tac."

He nodded in agreement. "We can't miss the plane to Honolulu."

Willie glanced at Matt, who stood braced against the brisk wind, hands in his pockets. "We still have plenty of time if we leave right away," she said. "We'll use Matt as the other witness."

He opened his mouth to protest, but she grabbed his arm. "You don't mind helping, do you?" she asked him, her smile curving laugh lines into her cheeks. "Think of the whole thing as a chance for future customers."

He peered into her face, not sure how to take her remark. To his surprise her eyes were sparkling with mirth. They were also greener than he'd noticed before. He forgot what he was about to say, and found himself nodding and grinning back at her, instead.

"Come on," she said, walking toward the plane before he had a chance for second thoughts.

The closer they got, the more unreliable the aircraft appeared to him.

"Is it safe?" he asked as she hustled him on board. "It looks like it was built in World War II."

"It's as safe as the car you came in," said the man who was sitting in the pilot's seat. He put on a set of headphones and began flipping levers.

Matt was thinking that the man's comparison was ill chosen, when the plane began to shake. Willie pulled him down beside her and snapped a seat belt shut across his flat middle.

"Suppose you tell me just what's going on," he said to her in an undertone after the plane had taken off and was climbing higher.

"John and Lisa are getting married in the air," she said. "No big deal."

Matt closed his eyes and slowly shook his head, reminding himself silently that his sister's happiness was worth any risk he might have to take.

A few moments later the plane leveled off. Willie stood and opened her bag. She shook out a dark blue robe and put it on over her clothes. The shiny material was appliquéd with silver moons and stars.

Very appropriate, Matt thought dryly.

"Like it?" she asked, whirling before him.

The plane hit a sudden air pocket and Matt was sure the expression on his face was answer enough. He'd rather be arguing a case for a bigamist than sitting where he was now.

The ceremony, which took place in the belly of the plane, was brief but rather touching. The emotion in the groom's voice when he repeated his vows made Matt uncomfortable. Grimly he wondered if the couple *would* end up in his office someday as Willie had laughingly suggested, as far apart as they were close now.

While he was mulling that thought over, the new bride and groom donned nylon jumpsuits and began to snap on parachutes. Matt's nervous gaze shifted from them to Willie and back. The fact that the other witness was also preparing for a rapid exit did nothing to reassure him.

When Willie opened the zipper down the front of her robe, Matt became even more nervous. She returned his stare with a devilish grin as she watched him pale beneath his tan.

"Ever done any skydiving?"

His mouth turned down at the corners and Willie realized it was time to stop teasing. He had gone up with them and she'd never thought to ask if he had an aversion to flying. Apparently if he did, he wasn't about to give in to it.

"Don't worry, man," the groom said. "Lisa and I wouldn't dream of letting you dive if you haven't had experience. Of course, if you've taken the training, you're welcome to join us."

"No, thanks," Matt said hastily, shaking John's hand. "And congratulations. Skydiving's probably a lot less dangerous than what you've just done."

John chuckled appreciatively, then went forward to check with the pilot. Willie finished folding her robe and put it back into the nylon bag. Then she sat down and began to fill out the marriage certificate. Matt marveled that she could manage such elaborate calligraphy despite the movement of the plane.

After everyone had signed in the appropriate places and John and Lisa had both thanked Matt for filling in, the other witness slid open the door. Matt quickly sat back down and strapped on his seat belt. In a few moments the bride and groom were gone, the plane bobbing slightly as they leaped into space.

The pilot banked in a lazy circle, and Willie pressed her nose to the window. She watched the young couple's descent as they drifted together, joined. Then they broke apart. First one chute, then the other opened, bright blobs of red, yellow and purple against the landscape far below.

"That's about how long most marriages last," Matt said, leaning forward to watch with her.

"They separated so their chutes wouldn't tangle," she told him. "My marriages last."

"Then why haven't you tried it yourself?" Matt asked as she turned away from the window to look at him.

"Skydiving? What makes you think I haven't?"

"Marriage. You seem so convinced it's the ultimate state for mankind."

"I will when the time is right," she said with confidence.

"Oh, yes. When your prince comes along."

"A commoner would do fine if he has the right qualities."

Matt was tempted to ask what they might be, but something held him back. With most women, he would have guessed the first requirement to be a big bank balance followed by a fancy house, but with Willie he had a suspicion that money wouldn't be first on the list. Maybe second or third.

"I believe in love, Mr. Bailey, or I wouldn't be in this business," Willie continued, as if she'd read his thoughts. "If I didn't believe wholeheartedly in what I do, I'd probably be practicing law in some musty office somewhere."

He couldn't help but grin as he looked down at her. "I doubt that," he said, his gaze drifting to her cloud of red hair before he returned his attention to her pixie face. "Wherever you were things would be pretty lively, I'll bet. Not musty at all."

Her cheeks turned pink, and Matt's own words surprised him. He wasn't given to compliments and he didn't even like her.

His words startled Willie, too. "Thank you, I think," she said. "But basically I'm a quiet person. Other than the occasional less traditional ceremony—" she gestured around them with an outstretched hand "—my life is pretty ordinary."

"I'll bet." His tone expressed frank disbelief as he glanced at the trim foot she was swinging back and forth. Then he returned his attention to her face. "When you're not wearing some outlandish robes that look like they've been designed for Merlin the Magician, you dress like a teenage baby-sitter. You have an aunt whose hair is the color of a punk rocker's, and you have more holes in your ears than anyone I've ever seen."

Willie absently felt the small row of gold balls that went up her earlobe, as she bit back a sharp retort. "You must have a pretty staid clientele," she said finally. "Multiple piercing is very much in style."

"So's nose piercing, but I haven't been tempted to try it," he drawled as the plane touched down on the grass runway.

"Too bad," she said under her breath. "It might have loosened you up a bit."

As they left the airport, Willie drove in silence, dreading what she was certain Matt wanted to talk about. After a few minutes she glanced over at him. He was staring straight ahead, and the hand resting on his muscular thigh was curled into a fist. For a moment Willie felt a sharp pang of pity for him, realizing why he was acting so tense. Amanda was defying him, probably for the first time, and the poor man was terrified of losing her.

"What did you want to discuss?" Willie urged, glancing at the road, then back at him. Might as well get it over with.

Matt sighed and raked a large hand through his dark hair, leaving it mussed and sexy looking, as if he'd just climbed out of bed. Willie tore her gaze away, banishing the thought and trying her best to concentrate on her driving.

"You probably already know. I want to talk about Amanda."

When Willie remained silent he continued, reeling off his arguments as if he were mentally ticking them off on his fingers. His voice was emotionless.

"She's too young to know what she wants," he said. "She hasn't dated that much and she has no basis of comparison."

"What would you have her do, Mr. Bailey?" Willie asked, not thinking about the fact that she'd been calling him "Matt" for a couple of hours. "Hang around a few singles' bars until she gets some experience?"

His brows bunched together into a frown. "Of course not. I want her to attend college, get a degree—"

"And date a dozen preppies with overactive libidos so she'll recognize the qualities in a man like Craig when she meets him," Willie finished for him. "Apparently she already knows." Willie wondered if, having been raised by someone as domineering as Matt, Amanda was subconsciously choosing in Craig a quiet, gentle husband as a pleasant change.

"What do you have against a college education?" Matt asked. "You've got one, and a law degree, or you wouldn't be a justice of the peace."

Willie hesitated. She couldn't disagree that it would be wonderful if Amanda were willing to go on to school. "She's made her choice," she said finally. "Whatever you and I think is best, it's Amanda's decision that counts."

"Have you ever refused to perform a wedding?" he asked. "For any reason?"

Willie nibbled on her lower lip. "Of course. A few months ago I turned down the chance to unite two people in a cemetery at midnight under a full moon. The entire wedding party was going to wear black and—" she shuddered at the memory "—they had written their own vows."

"Is that the only one?"

She continued thoughtfully. "I do try to talk to the parties for a few minutes, just to make sure they're serious and committed. There isn't really time to counsel them, though, so I mainly go on instinct."

Matt snorted, and Willie's hands tightened on the steering wheel.

"I don't marry people who are under age and don't have the proper permission, or if they don't have the necessary paperwork...." She looked over at him and saw that he was frowning darkly. "I even stopped a ceremony once when the bride and groom got into an argument. He thought her tone of voice was 'frivolous,' and when she finally slapped him I suggested they take some time to reconsider." She glanced at him, unable to resist a smile. "They got counseling and I married them some months later. Now they have two children and I still get Christmas cards."

Beside her Matt shifted impatiently. "What about insanity?" he asked. "Mental illness?"

Willie chuckled. "I figured you thought all my clients were suffering from that." Her tone was full of amusement.

Ignoring her smile, he said, "Amanda and that—"

Willie gave him a sharp look.

"That boy," he continued, frowning fiercely, "are getting into another fiasco this weekend. I want you to talk her out of it."

"No."

Clearly Matthew Bailey wasn't used to being turned down. "No?" he echoed.

Willie shook her head, slowing for a turn. "They're in love," she said. "I can't interfere if they don't ask me to."

"Can't or won't?"

She took one hand off the wheel and patted Matt's clenched fist in what she'd meant to be a comforting gesture. A jolt of electricity ran up her arm and she snatched her hand back, trying to remember his last question.

"Can't," she repeated firmly. "I'm not a marriage counselor, and Amanda hasn't asked my opinion."

Matt muttered a swear word under his breath. "Your head is filled with cotton candy," he said gruffly. "And romantic drivel that belongs in fairy tales."

Willie was beginning to lose her temper. "Love between two people attracted to each other isn't drivel," she exclaimed hotly.

"No," he agreed. "It's hormones."

Willie almost missed the turn into her driveway. "What?"

"When you've parked the car, I'll show you."

Willie pulled into a small lot in front of her wedding chapel and parked at one end. She shut off the engine and turned to the man beside her. "Show me what?" she asked, curious despite her growing annoyance.

With a smile that could only be called pure devilment, he pulled her to him. "This," he muttered.

Willie barely had time to close her mouth before he covered it with his. Big hands held her arms as his lips brushed hers in a surprisingly tender caress. The tang of his cologne tickled her nostrils. Her fingers, as if they'd sprouted a will of their own, curled into the soft fabric of his coat as her head began to spin. When it came to kissing, Matt was clearly an expert.

As Willie went limp against him, Matt molded her mouth to his, increasing the pressure of his lips gradually. Willie thought her lungs would burst. When a moan of reaction floated up from her throat, he lifted away fractionally and she sucked in a gulp of air. Then, with an indecipherable murmur, he kissed her again.

This time she felt the tip of his tongue trace the outline of her mouth, searing her like a flame. His arms tightened around her in the cramped confines of the car and her lips parted beneath his insistence. Just when she felt that her whole body was about to turn into a mindless, throbbing pool of ecstasy, he released her abruptly.

His breathing was shallow and rapid and his eyes were almost black as Willie stared at him, trying to focus.

"See?" he said harshly as she touched her tingling lips with tentative fingers.

Willie sighed, regarding Matt with a wholly new light. No man had ever made her feel as he had, excited and shaky, hot and cold all at the same time.

"See what?" she murmured softly, noticing the way his face had flushed beneath his tan.

"Hormones," he snapped. "There's nothing romantic about what just happened between us. I haven't had a woman in quite a while and you're reasonably attractive, if a little offbeat. I don't love you and you don't love me, but I bet your pulse isn't normal. I know mine sure as hell isn't. Without animal lust our race would have died out long ago."

"Stop!" Willie cried as her frustration turned to fury. It was either convert the emotion that filled her into a blast of temper or dissolve into a puddle of humiliation. His words had sliced through the rosy haze of her response like the blade of a sword, making her feel like a kid with an unrequited crush.

"I really pity your sister," Willie blazed at him. "You're such a twisted person. You, you…" She was so angry that she sputtered helplessly, unable to think of a description dire enough, black enough, to use. She clenched her fists and blinked back tears of frustration, wishing for once that she hadn't been raised by a minister, that she'd paid more attention to some of the words the other kids had used and she had scrupulously avoided.

"You—jerk!" she finally shouted for lack of anything stronger.

Matt was looking at her with an unreadable expression on his face. Willie suddenly realized that her very overreaction was a dead giveaway to how strongly his kiss had affected her. Taking a deep breath, she grabbed her duffel bag and got out of her car.

"Does this mean you won't talk to Amanda?" he asked after he'd unfolded his big body and was standing facing her across the dusty hood of the Corvair. "Isn't there any way I can convince you that letting Amanda marry that bum would be a mistake?"

Willie glared at him. As he stared back, she thought she saw something in his eyes beneath all the cynicism. It could be loneliness, perhaps fear. Or it could be a trick of the light. Willie was still too angry to care which.

If Matt Bailey had forgotten how wonderful love could be, she certainly wasn't the one to remind him. They didn't even like each other.

Matt glanced again at his watch, realizing he'd never called his office. He'd do it from his car. "Are you going to give me an answer or not?" he demanded impatiently.

"I can't interfere unless Amanda asks for my advice."

Giving her a last look that would have wilted spinach, Matt turned on his well-polished heel and stalked to his white Continental. Before he could drive off, Willie ran lightly up the steps, yanked open the front door and dashed into her house, slamming it behind her.

As he peeled out of the parking area and onto Aurora Avenue, Matt had to consciously loosen his grip on the steering wheel. Willie Webster was one stubborn, mixed-up woman, he fumed silently. Then after a moment a reluctant grin tugged at his mouth as he recalled the way she'd lit into him. She'd enjoyed that kiss as much as he had, and she'd been furious at what he'd said about hormones.

For a minute he wished things were different, but then the problems with his sister pounded back into his head. Remembrance of the upcoming disaster and his inability to forestall it made him swear out loud as he pressed down on the accelerator of his Lincoln. The car responded smoothly, carrying Matt past the parked police car at a good twenty miles over the posted limit.

WHEN WILLIE STOMPED into the kitchen, Aunt Violet was already there. "Want some tea, dear?" she asked. "It's peppermint. Good for what ails you."

"And what exactly ails me?" Willie asked testily as she took the bone china cup and saucer her aunt handed her. Today Violet's hair was untinted, as white as cotton fluff. She wore a print dress, and from her ears dangled enameled replicas of the Space Needle.

"That man who tore out of here," Violet said, taking her own cup to the parlor. "I'd love to get a look at his palm."

A slight chill shivered across Willie's skin as she wondered what else Violet had seen. If she suspected any kind of attraction between Willie and Matt, which of course there wasn't, she'd sink her teeth into it like a pit bull with a rump roast. Violet was constantly checking the cards for any sign of a man in Willie's future, deploring the fact that in Willie's line of work, practically the only ones she met were almost instantly ineligible.

Willie cast about uncomfortably for something that would throw off Violet's suspicions.

"The only thing Matthew Bailey's interested in is stopping his sister's wedding," she said. "He's hardly in the market for one of his own."

Violet snorted. "Since when do men know what's good for them, or even what they want until some woman shows them?" Violet freely admitted having proposed to the man she had been blissfully married to for many years. After she was widowed she'd come to keep house for Willie's father, the minister. Perhaps the name Violet was misleading; when it came to men she was anything but shy and had several gentlemen friends to prove it.

"Maybe it's time you were thinking about remarrying yourself," Willie suggested a little desperately. "What about that nice Bill Clancy, who took you to bingo last Tuesday night?"

Violet set her cup down with a clatter of annoyance. "Bill Clancy's so set in his ways he'd drive me crazy. His daily routine is chiseled in concrete. He eats the same dinner on the same night every week and he even wears the same shirt on the same day—blue plaid on Wednesday, green stripe on Friday."

She stopped and took a deep breath. "He probably takes a bath on Saturday night if he needs it or not, and if we were married that's the only night we'd—" she glanced at Willie, then down at her teacup "—cuddle," she finished after a delicate pause.

"Well, what about Clarence Twitty or that Rudy person who always calls you?" Willie was determined to keep Violet's attention away from Matt and herself.

"Can you picture me married to a man named Twitty?" Aunt Violet demanded, eyes flashing behind her wire-framed glasses. "Perhaps I should go with one of those new hyphenated surnames, and wouldn't that be dignified?" asked the woman whose last name had been Dibble ever since Willie had know her.

Willie contemplated what the results of such a merger would be, and couldn't help but smile.

"And all Rudy cares about is my double fudge chocolate cake," Violet continued with a sniff. "If I gave him the recipe I'd probably never see the man again."

"Perhaps you're being too picky," Willie suggested, unable to resist the chance to needle the older woman a little more. Violet had certainly given Willie a bundle of unsolicited advice over the past few years, gleaned from her tarot cards and Willie's own palm whenever Violet could grab it.

"I don't have time to pursue this," Violet said impatiently, standing and picking up her cup and saucer. "I have a reading in half an hour."

Willie smiled to herself. One way to distract Violet from Willie's single state was to zero in on Violet's own. Willie would have to remember that, and had a feeling she'd need the defensive maneuver until Amanda's wedding was over and Matt Bailey was out of her life for good.

"CAN'T I at least keep my horse?" asked the man who sat across from Matt in his luxurious law office.

Matt studied his client, noticing not for the first time the unflattering toupee and the unhealthy flush to his complexion, both of which Matt decided were brought on by the pressures of being married to a much younger woman.

"You gave her the horse in front of at least a hundred witnesses," Matt reminded him. "Right after he won the Longacres Mile last year." Matt sat back in his burgundy leather executive chair and steepled his fingers beneath his chin. Pity for the man who sat across from him, wiping a perspiring brow with a hand-monogrammed handkerchief, didn't soften Matt's tone. He pitied all the clients who refused to learn.

"I never could have believed that Coral would do this to me," Arthur Fenton said, shaking his head. "I was sure she loved me."

What she loved was your money, Matt thought, striving to keep his expression impassive. He'd done everything he could to persuade Arthur and his bride to sign a prenuptial agreement when the man had announced his upcoming marriage to a part-time singer-dancer—and, in Matt's opinion, full-time gold digger—thirty years his junior.

Had Arthur listened? No, of course not. He'd been too dazzled by Coral's assets to give any thought to protecting his own. Now, after only two and a half years of marriage, Coral had left him for their horse trainer. And she was asking for enough money to support them both.

Matt drummed his fingers on the surface of his desk. It was all he could do to resist reminding the other man how much the last divorce had cost him, but he managed to bite back the words. Perhaps the next time Arthur would heed his advice about a prenuptial agreement.

"Give her whatever she has coming," Arthur said after emitting a long, mournful sigh. He stubbed his cigarette out in the brass ashtray on the corner of Matt's desk and quickly lit up another. After taking a deep drag that set off a series of barking coughs, he dabbed at his eyes and muttered, "See if she'll sell me back the damned horse. He's won two important races in California already this season."

Arthur stood and leaned over Matt's desk, his ample girth sagging. "Next time I'll listen," he said in a softer voice, "and I'll sign your damned agreement."

Matt remembered that he'd said the same thing after his second divorce, but refrained from reminding him. "I'll call you," he said, clapping the shorter man on the shoulder as he preceded Matt to the door. "And I'll keep the damage to an absolute minimum."

"Yeah," Arthur said around his cigarette. "Leave me enough to pay your bill."

Matt laughed at the attempted joke, nodded and watched Arthur's departing figure. He didn't know which was worse—the repeat customer who never learned, or the middle-aged wife who came to him, stunned and bewildered, when her spouse of thirty or forty years left because someone else made him feel younger, or the couple who fought over custody of the children they'd once created in love with the same greed they did the house or the cars. At least he and Michelle hadn't had any kids to fight over.

Matt stood at the window with its view of other skyscrapers and glimpses of Elliot Bay to the west. Was that what lay ahead for Amanda and her Craig—a few years of scrimping on service pay, too many babies too soon, then a painful divorce?

"No!" He almost jumped when he realized he'd said the word aloud. Damn that Willie Webster for refusing to talk some sense into his sister.

He'd talked to Amanda himself every night that week, and the rescheduled ceremony was drawing ever closer. Amanda had gotten paler and quieter each day, but he had no idea whether he was getting through to her. If only she'd wait, go to college, meet some other men. He had no doubt that she'd find her classes and a campus full of intelligent male students more interesting than that shy little weasel she wanted to marry.

Matt slammed his fist into his open palm. Tonight was Friday. He planned to take Amanda to a really posh restaurant just to show her the kind of thing she'd be missing on a sailor's salary.

What a break it was that her fiancé had been unable to get away from the base all week. The commander had granted him another weekend pass on the condition he pull extra duty. Matt knew he'd called Amanda several times, but that was all. If Matt couldn't get through to her tonight, he'd have to give up.

THE DAY of Amanda's wedding dawned sunny and unseasonably warm. Willie had three ceremonies before the Bailey-Preston nuptials, then a small break to freshen up and to gird herself against Matt's hostility. He'd phoned twice during the week, but Violet had fielded his calls.

Willie wondered how Amanda was holding up under the pressure he must be exerting, and hoped he wasn't damaging his relationship with her more surely than any marriage would.

When he'd called the first time, Matt had said something to Violet about a speeding ticket, which he seemed to blame on Willie. Willie didn't understand how it could be her fault, and Violet had been vague about the details.

As Willie was finishing a cup of licorice tea and a slice of homemade bread while she prepared for the day's schedule, the phone rang in the living room. Violet answered, adjusting the collar of her green paisley dress, as Willie took a last swallow and pushed back her chair.

"The telephone's for you, dear."

Before Willie could ask who it was, the front bell pealed. "I'll get that," Violet said, patting her light green hair. "You take care of your call."

Willie picked up the receiver and had barely uttered a greeting, when Matt's deep voice interrupted. "Willie, I'm at my wit's end," he said. "Amanda's gone."

3

WILLIE GRIPPED the receiver tighter. "How long has Amanda been gone?"

Matt's voice was rigidly controlled. "I don't know. When she didn't come down I knocked on her door to see if she wanted some breakfast. There was no sign of her, and her friend Melodie is due to arrive any minute to help her get ready for the wedding."

Willie took a deep breath, trying to think. "Maybe she's gone for a walk," she suggested, "or running an errand. She could have forgotten to get something—"

"No, no." His voice cut impatiently across hers. "I've been up for hours and she would have had to sneak by me to leave."

The worry in his voice reached out to Willie, making her wish she were there to hold his hand, to stroke the unruly strands of hair off his wide forehead. Good Lord, what was she thinking? Matt didn't need nor want her to fuss over him. With a frown she focused her attention on the problem, trying to be hopeful.

"There's plenty of time yet," she said finally, wishing there were something else she could give him, something stronger to hold on to. "I'm sure she'll be back soon."

"Damn," he swore. "There's the door. It's probably her ditzy girlfriend. Hold on a second."

"Maybe she knows something," Willie said before he set down the receiver. The snort he uttered in response was hardly encouraging, but she tried to remind herself that he was upset.

In a moment he was back on the line and his tone was one of suppressed fury. "It was a messenger. Amanda and Craig have eloped, and she asked me to call you to break their appointment."

Willie was speechless with surprise. She hadn't expected anything like this. "Does she say why?"

There was another long pause, then he answered in an expressionless tone. "Yeah, she says why, but I don't want to go into this on the telephone."

The deadness in his voice made Willie ache for him, and she frowned as she recalled her full schedule. "I have the time of your sister's, uh, appointment free," she said, stumbling over the reminder she was sure would rub salt into Matt's wounds. "Could you come over here then?"

"Why?"

Good question. "We could talk. Perhaps I can help." In truth, she felt totally helpless, but hated to think of him sitting alone, waiting, while the minutes ticked by.

"I want to stay here in case she calls."

She hadn't thought about that, but he was right. "What about later? Will you keep me posted?" Willie pressed. At the moment she was more worried about Matt than she was about Amanda. The younger girl had Craig to take care of her, and Matt had no one. Or maybe she was leaping to conclusions. A man as handsome and successful as Matthew Bailey undoubtedly had any number of someones.

"Is there a friend you can call?" she asked before he'd had a chance to answer her other questions.

"Call for what?" His voice had turned sullen.

"Someone to be with you," she said, "to keep you company while you wait."

When he spoke again, his voice had softened slightly. "Thank you for your concern, but I'll be okay. If I hear anything more I'll let you know." There was a pause and then he startled her with his next request. "Would you be free to have dinner with me?"

Ignoring the bubble of excitement that rose within her, Willie flipped through her book. "I have a wedding at eight o'clock at the Marine View Country Club," she said, "but I'm free for two hours before that."

"Okay." She thought she heard relief in his voice, but wasn't sure. "I don't want to tie up the line now, so I'll get back to you," he added.

"Okay. I'll—"

He'd hung up.

Fuming, Willie glared at the receiver. Just when she'd thought he was opening up to her a little, he'd retreated behind that impenetrable shell of arrogance. Not that she should care if he was hurting, even if the memory of his kiss did evoke warm feelings in her.

No, that wasn't right. He was a fellow human being and he was apparently alone and needy. For now that was all that was important. Willie could sort out the way he made her feel some other time, when she didn't have a parade of blissful lovebirds waiting to be united in matrimony. Too bad Matthew Bailey didn't have as much faith in that commitment as she did; he might accept his sister's actions with less fear and resentment.

"Hurry up, dear," Aunt Violet said from the kitchen. "The Purdy-Ledbetter party will be here any minute."

AFTER HE'D ANSWERED the door again, quizzed Amanda's friend Melodie carefully, then sent her away, Matt reread Amanda's note. Then he turned to the small bar in the corner of the vast living room. He couldn't remember the last time he'd had a drink at nine-thirty in the morning, but this seemed like an excellent time to indulge.

He poured a single measure of Scotch into a short lead-crystal glass and sank into one of the two gray leather couches that faced each other across a table of smoked glass and driftwood. The crumpled note was stuffed into his shirt pocket.

Apparently he hadn't been as subtle as he'd thought all week with his suggestions that Amanda rethink the step she was taking and his comments about the opportunities that awaited an intelligent young woman with a college degree.

Matt took a sip of the smooth liquor, hardly noticing as it slid down his throat. He reached for the note again, then dropped his hand. There was no need to refresh his memory; the words were already burned into his brain.

In neatly rounded letters Amanda had written:

I'm sorry I can't do what you want.
To spare you any more discomfort, Craig and I have decided to elope.
Don't worry.

Love, Mandy

P. S. Please cancel our appointment and apologize to Willie for us.

Matt raked a trembling hand through his hair and finished the Scotch in one gulp.

"Don't worry." What a laugh! He'd been worried about her since she was nine years old and enshrouded in grief over their parents' sudden and pointless deaths, and he wasn't about to stop just because she told him to.

He let his head rest against the back of the couch as he remembered. He'd been in the middle of a complicated case for an important client when Amanda had gone off to camp that summer, a pale, subdued little ghost. He'd barely had time to deal with his own grief, let alone be of any help to her. To his surprise and relief, she'd come back after two months of Willie's friendship and protection a different girl, not quite the laughing imp she'd been before the accident but not the sad little shadow who'd left with drooping shoulders, either. The healing had begun.

He'd always meant to go and meet the "Willie" person she'd chattered about so incessantly, but there had never been time, and after a while he'd forgotten all about her. Too bad he'd been so stacked up with work that summer and had never gotten up to the camp, or he would have met Willie then.

Idly he wondered if he would have felt the same attraction he did now. Then he mentally pulled himself up short. Willie was a hopeless romantic, a muzzy-headed dreamer he had no time for. He'd kissed her once to prove a point. Just because the kiss had proved to be unexpectedly pleasurable was nothing personal.

Somewhere deep inside, his logical lawyer's mind began to protest his reasoning, but he steadfastly ignored the niggling inner voice.

Matt rose and wandered into the immaculate kitchen, empty glass in hand. What did he care that he'd never met Willie before now? There was no reason to see her again, since Amanda wasn't getting married at her tacky little chapel. The building was painted pink, for God's sake, with a fake wishing well in the front yard and a neon sign that flashed on and off. As different from his cedar-and-tinted-glass law office as two businesses could be, and a far cry from the setting he'd pictured for his sister's wedding some years down the road, when she was old enough to know what she was doing.

Rinsing out the glass, he remembered that he'd offered to take Willie to dinner that evening. Well, it would be simple enough to cancel. He turned to call, then stopped. If he hadn't heard from Amanda by then, Willie's company might make the time go faster. They could order in so he wouldn't miss Amanda's call.

No. He shook his head. If he wanted companionship, he had an address book full of numbers. Women who knew how to play sophisticated games, who could distract him with entertaining but meaningless conversation; women who wouldn't dream of prying into his personal thoughts. And, he told himself with a sour little twist to his lips, women who sure as hell wouldn't pepper him with insults or look at him with an expression that clearly said they were laughing behind their hands. Women who might not want him sprawled on the carpet unless they were there under him.

He wandered restlessly out onto the redwood deck, barely glancing toward the lakeshore at the foot of his spacious back lawn. What did he need with an uptight little virgin who lived in a pink house and used a perfectly good law degree to perform weddings?

A picture of Willie floated past his consciousness, red curls in a flaming halo, ears twinkling with rows of tiny hoops. Perhaps "uptight" wasn't quite the right word. She hadn't been uptight when he'd kissed her. She had been responsive, openly enjoying what had sprung between them as much as he had. She probably wasn't a virgin, either.

The memory of the shared kiss was doing uncomfortable things to him, making Matt swear violently as he went back into the house. He glared at the silent telephone. *Call, dammit,* he willed Amanda silently.

EACH TIME THE PHONE RANG at Willie's she hoped it would be Matt with news of Amanda, but it never was. When her last couple left, hands linked and faces glowing, she dialed Matt's number. When he answered she hesitated, hating to dash the hope in his voice.

"It's Willie Webster," she said. "I guess you haven't heard anything."

"No."

"You sound tired. Perhaps we should cancel—"

"I'd really like to see you, if you don't mind coming here," he cut in quickly. There was a wistful note in his deep voice that Willie was certain would infuriate him if he'd been aware of it.

"'Here'? I mean, at your house?" His request rattled her. Somehow she'd pictured herself bolstering his spirits in a much more public setting.

"We can order in. I want to be home in case Amanda calls."

Of course. She hadn't been thinking.

"Okay. Give me directions." Willie thrust aside her reservations and the sharp little prick of guilt. She was going to Matt's house on a mission of mercy, not because she wanted to see him alone or because she was hoping he might kiss her again. When her eyes met their knowing reflection in the mirror, Willie turned her back. At least Aunt Violet wasn't there to question the flush of color in her cheeks.

IMPRESSED by the exclusive neighborhood, Willie drove up the paved driveway to Matt's house on the shore of Lake Washington. Even though it was in the heart of a long-established area, his house turned out to be a perfect blend of modern and traditional, its elegant yet simple lines broken by a series of outdoor decks and a multilevel tiled roof.

Willie parked her Corvair before the carved double front doors with their matching stained glass windows and slid nervously from the front seat. Since the wedding she was performing that evening was a formal affair and an eminently traditional one, with ten bridesmaids and an equal number of groomsmen, she was dressed in a neat blue suit instead of one of her usual flowing caftans. The jacket's tailored style above a slim skirt gave her an extra layer of confidence as she took a deep breath and boldly swung the brass knocker engraved with the letter *B*.

Chimes sounded somewhere within the house, and heavy footsteps approached. Willie wet her lips with her tongue as one massive door swung back on silent hinges. A rainbow of color from the stained glass window fell on Matt's face as he gazed at her without a smile or a word.

After an awkward moment, Willie shifted from one foot to the other. "Can I come in?"

He smiled, and his face was transformed. "I'm sorry," he said as he stepped back and made a gesture of welcome with his hand.

Matt was wearing a white shirt, open at the neck with the sleeves rolled up on his muscular forearms, and tight-fitting jeans, softened by many washings and faded by whatever method was currently popular to a worn and uneven gray. His black boots looked as though they'd been chosen for comfort rather than style. They were scuffed and scratched, adding another couple of inches to his already impressive height.

Even in her two-inch heels, Willie was sure she was getting a crick in her neck from looking up. Trust Matt Bailey to give her a pain there, she thought as she turned to face him, purse held in front of her like some kind of shield.

His presence before her almost distracted Willie from noticing the splendor of the entry hall, but not quite. The floor was polished wood, with the individual boards fit together in a complicated pattern that enhanced the fine grain. Above their heads the ceiling soared away and a modern chandelier caught the light from the tall windows. Willie made a mental note to look more closely at a later time.

"Mandy called a few minutes ago," Matt said as they went into a living room that could have been featured in a decorating magazine.

Willie swiveled toward him. "When are they coming back?"

"Tomorrow."

Without thinking she reached out and patted his muscular forearm. His skin was warm and the dark hairs tickled the sensitive pads of her fingers. The gesture that had been meant as a comfort turned into something else.

"I'm sure that everything will work out," she said, trying to keep the reaction from her voice. "Do you feel better now that you've talked to her?"

His brooding expression and defeated tone told her a great deal. "They're married, aren't they?" He shrugged his big shoulders. "I guess I have to accept it."

"That would be the best thing. Otherwise you may lose Amanda for good."

Matt looked down at the woman who stood before him in a trim little suit. Her gray-green eyes were wide and her lips were slightly parted. He understood what she was trying to say—don't force Amanda to choose between you and Craig. The new bride was going to have enough adjustments to make without her brother putting any more pressure on her. He had to respect Willie for saying what she thought, instead of mouthing a platitude to make him feel better.

"Right," he said, "but if Preston doesn't treat her right, I'll tear him apart."

Willie bobbed her head, apricot-colored curls swirling. "Fine," she breathed on a sigh of relief. "Just make sure you have your facts straight before you go barging in like the Green Berets, okay?"

Matt grinned reluctantly, tempted to ask if she always said exactly what she was thinking. "Would I do that?" he asked, instead.

She returned his smile. "Somehow I can picture you doing just that."

"Okay," he agreed. "I'll do my best. I'm sure Mandy will come to her senses soon, anyway, but I wish you had been willing to talk to her." He picked up a printed brochure. "Let's order dinner. How do you feel about pizza and imported beer?"

Willie felt another sharp jab of guilt. Doing her best to ignore it along with his cynical view of the longevity of Amanda's marriage, she turned her attention to the take-out list. She was dying to ask him more about Amanda's note, but restrained her curiosity.

"I have a wedding at eight," she said, "so I'd better skip the beer. Do you have any diet soda?"

MATT HAD SHOWN Willie the rest of the house while they waited for the food to be delivered. It was easy to see that he was proud of it, but Willie was surprised to learn that he had done a lot of the remodeling himself.

She'd pictured him behind a massive desk, slicing through the bonds of matrimony with dark-humored enthusiasm; now the image altered to one of him stripped to the waist and wielding a hammer. the new image was a lot tougher on her own awakened senses. Willie rubbed damp palms together as she followed him back to the main floor, trying hard not to focus on the width of his powerful shoulders as he preceded her.

He'd led the conversation through a series of subjects while they ate, and Willie was surprised to find that a lot of their tastes were similar. They both liked plays, especially musicals, and they'd each been to see the same exhibit of blown-glass sculpture currently at a small gallery in the north end.

Willie admitted she was an earnest Mariners baseball fan, and Matt confessed that he watched professional wrestling on late-night television, as well as being a staunch Seahawks football fan. While Matt had gotten his law degree back East, Willie had attended the University of Washington right in Seattle. They had something else in common, too. They'd each waited tables while they'd done undergraduate work.

By the time Willie had finished her last piece of pizza and delicately licked her fingers, she felt as if she knew a great deal more about Matt, but not the things that made him tick.

"I appreciate the way you looked after Mandy that first summer," he said, draining his beer glass. "And you kept writing to her all these years. Not many teenagers would have taken the time for someone so much younger."

"Amanda was always special to me," Willie replied, glancing at her watch. "I enjoyed seeing her begin to come out of her shell after a while, but it would have helped if you could have made it up for a parents' day." She still remembered Amanda's pinched face as the other girls had sat around the campfire with their families and Amanda had huddled next to Willie.

Matt shifted uncomfortably. "I was working on a big case at the time."

Willie didn't respond.

Matt wasn't used to anyone questioning his motives, even with the silent but easily read look Willie gave him.

"Besides, she had you."

"I wasn't family." She hadn't meant to lose her temper, but his lack of understanding had provoked her.

Matt rose and began to pace. "I was young myself," he said. "Fresh out of law school and scrambling to build a practice. Our parents were killed on the way home from a party. According to some of the other guests, they'd been arguing all evening and had both been drinking." He slammed a fist into his open palm. "It was so unnecessary," he gritted. "They fought like cats and dogs, but they couldn't stay apart."

"Perhaps they loved each other," Willie couldn't help commenting.

"Love!" His tone was derisive. "If that's love . . ."

"Maybe, maybe not. I see love every day, and it comes in many forms." Willie's voice softened. Had Matt never experienced its wonders? She remembered briefly the stories her father had told her about the mother she never knew, the wife he had loved so much. Willie firmly believed in the kind of love that would last a lifetime.

Matt turned to glare down at her. "I see the results of that misguided emotion every day, lady," he said on a snarl. "I see the lives it twists and hurts, and I'd say it's a vastly overrated commodity."

Willie stood. "You only see one side—" she began.

He raised a detaining hand. "I saw my parents. I even tried the blessed state myself. Nothing you can say will convince me it's more than overactive hormones or a greedy quest for security."

Willie was speechless with shock at his cynicism. "You're dismissing the attraction, the satisfaction, the shared goals two people in love can enjoy. Millions of couples live that love every day."

For a moment Matt was silent as they stared at each other, emotions running high.

"Willie," he murmured, pulling her close. "You are truly beautiful when you're defending your romantic notions so passionately." He lowered his head. "I want that passion."

Willie took a step back and her calf hit the edge of the couch. His fingers tightened on her arms, and she remembered the way his mouth had felt against hers the last time he'd kissed her. The resistance flowed out of her, to be replaced by a new kind of tension.

When he touched his lips to hers, she didn't pull away; she let her hands slide up his shoulders and around his neck. With a mutter of approval Matt pulled her closer as he molded her mouth with his.

For a long moment Matt submerged himself in the sweetness of her taste, the fragrance of her scent and the warmth of her embrace. He gathered her closer, lifting his mouth to string a row of kisses down her cheek to the graceful line of her throat. Willie's scent was stronger there, more heated and more intimate, as Matt buried his face in her hair.

Willie felt the tremor that rippled through him as they stood pressed together. Her lips tingled from his passionate kiss and her greedy hands urged his chin up. As his mouth returned to feast on hers his arms held her in a tight embrace.

The tiny, insistent voice of reason told Willie to pull back, to resist the potency of his touch, his taste. Willie barely heard that voice, but she did hear the faint pinging of her watch alarm reminding her of the wedding she was to perform in a mere half-hour.

Gasping for breath, she pushed at him. Matt had lifted his head when the alarm went off, and he was looking down at her with clouded eyes.

"What the hell is that?" His voice was rough, his face flushed.

"My—my watch," Willie stammered. "I have to go."

Matt swore colorfully. "Just like Cinderella," he said. "Will you turn into a pumpkin?"

Ignoring the inaccuracy of his questions, Willie swallowed and shook her head. He looked like a pirate, dark eyes narrowed, hair falling across his forehead. Lips—

She groaned, grasping for the composure that had slipped away and shattered around her. "The wedding I'm supposed to officiate at could turn into a riot if I'm late," she said, forcing calm into her voice. "There are twenty attendants, two flower girls, a ring bearer and a mother of the bride who hyperventilates in the face of emergency."

She ticked off the members of the wedding party on her fingers as she spoke, to give herself a moment. Matt was like a potent drug, and she could very easily become an addict.

"I get the message."

He was staring at her mouth, and the blistering heat of his gaze made Willie lick her lips with the tip of her tongue.

Matt sucked in a breath and reached for her, the expression in his eyes screened by thick lashes. "Come here."

Willie slumped against him, then quickly recovered as she remembered the time. With mixed feelings she struggled to avoid the descent of his head.

Remembering the way she'd sent him to the floor once before, Matt released her. There were only so many falls a man's pride could take, and he wasn't about to add another ignominious tumble to the list. He smothered his disappointment with irritation.

"Well," he snapped as she continued to stare, "why aren't you going?"

"Will you be okay?" Willie asked, the green of her eyes intensified by some emotion Matt couldn't begin to read.

For some reason her concern angered him. He didn't want her mothering; he wanted her. . . . That was the problem—he wanted her. Unwilling to deal with the feelings rushing through him, Matt once again gripped her upper arm and hustled her toward the front door.

"It wouldn't do for you to be late," he said as he opened the massive panel.

On the front step Willie turned to face him, confused by his abrupt change of mood. One moment he'd been kissing her passionately, the next he'd given her the bum's rush.

"Thanks for dinner," she said as the door swung shut.

She thought he'd answered before it closed completely, but couldn't be sure. What an unpredictable man.

Glancing at her watch, Willie gave a small shriek and ran to her car, doing her best to straighten the collar of her blouse and fluff out her hair as she started the engine. Being late to your own wedding was one thing, but the justice of the peace being late was inexcusable.

As she drove back down the long driveway, Matt watched her from behind the window's sheer drapery. He should be glad she was gone, relieved that their paths probably would not cross again. Instead he felt an unfamiliar emotion that had no place in his busy life. He felt very much alone.

WHEN AMANDA AND CRAIG arrived the next morning, relief temporarily crowded out the other emotions surging in Matt. He swept his sister into a bear hug, then managed to shake Craig's hand and congratulate him.

Matt was sure his expression was far from friendly as they clasped hands, but the younger man stood firm, accepting the words somberly, and Matt felt a grudging admiration for him. Matt knew how intimidating he could be; it was a demeanor he'd actively cultivated in the courtroom and across the bargaining table.

"How are you?" Amanda asked him nervously as they went into the house. "You're not angry."

Matt shoved his hands into the pockets of his khaki slacks. "Not angry, Amanda. A little hurt, and quite surprised."

She sighed and Craig stepped closer, putting a protective arm around her waist. Matt's mouth turned down at the corners when he saw the gesture for what it was. They were a unit now, standing together against any threat. He felt extraneous, usurped.

"We didn't mean to hurt you," Amanda said, her voice shaky. "All last week you kept trying to wear me down. I thought this would be the best way for all of us."

Matt started to protest, then recalled the campaign he had waged—the *subtle* campaign—and winced. Willie had been right to refuse to talk to Amanda. He sighed deeply, then turned to the bucket of champagne he'd put on ice earlier.

"Perhaps you were right," he said, setting out glasses. "Time will tell, won't it?" His inquiring gaze took in Craig as well as his sister. It was clear from the younger man's frown that he understood what Matt was implying, even if Amanda did not.

"Let's drink to your happiness." Matt felt slightly ashamed. He really did want Amanda to be happy and to come out of this mess in one piece. He made a silent vow to be there for her this time when she needed him, no matter what case was on his calendar.

"Craig and I have been talking," Amanda said as she sipped the bubbly champagne. "We'd like to have a small reception."

Matt raised one thick brow. "Oh?" When they'd first discussed the ceremony, Amanda hadn't been interested in any kind of special preparations. At the time Matt had assumed she was still wavering between going through with the marriage or not, and he hadn't pressed her.

"What changed your mind?"

She glanced at Craig before answering. "We'd like our friends *and* family—" she reached out to take Matt's hand in hers "—to share in our happiness. Craig's relatives are so far away, and we do plan to visit them when we can, but we want all our friends to meet one another." She cast a glowing smile at Craig.

"It wouldn't be anything elaborate," she went on. "Some people from the base, my friends from the library and, of course, Willie."

Matt's brows pinched together into a frown. "Willie?"

"Oh, yes. We wouldn't think to exclude her. If it wasn't for Willie, we might not be here together at all. It was her idea that Craig and I elope."

4

MATT FORCED HIMSELF to take a deep breath. "Let me get this straight," he said carefully, holding back the rage that threatened to consume him. "It was Willie's idea that you elope?"

Amanda smiled and nodded. "Yes. I mean, no."

For once her musical laugh grated on Matt's patience, making him clench his teeth.

"What I mean is," she continued, sending a warm smile in Craig's direction, "she didn't actually suggest that we elope."

Matt slowly let out the breath he'd been holding and relaxed his jaw. Perhaps he wouldn't throttle Willie, after all. At least, not right away.

"What exactly did she say?" he asked in a tight voice.

Craig, who must have been more aware than Amanda of the tension in the room, spoke up.

"She told Amanda to follow her heart," he said.

"That's right," she chimed in. "And we want her at our reception." Suddenly her expression clouded over and she began to chew anxiously on a fingernail. "You don't think her feelings are hurt that she didn't marry us, do you, Matt?"

As always, his annoyance melted away when he saw the worry in her eyes. He reached out a reassuring hand to pat her thin shoulder.

"I'm sure she understands," he said. "After all, you were just following her advice."

His words were rewarded by the immediate return of Amanda's sweet smile. "Of course," she agreed. "Willie will understand."

Matt was still angry with Willie for her meddling. She had refused to become involved when he had asked— no, begged—her to, claiming scruples that he considered misplaced, but she wasn't above dishing out unasked-for advice on her own.

Matt found himself looking forward to the chance of telling her in person that she was an interfering busybody whose rose-colored glasses needed cleaning.

"I DON'T THINK Amanda had me in mind when she told you to bring a guest," Aunt Violet was saying to Willie as they walked up the steps to Matt's house. She paused to look around at the beautifully landscaped front yard as Willie shifted the present they had brought—home-grown herbs in beautifully cut jars—and raised the heavy brass door knocker.

"Nonsense." Willie smoothed her full skirt and took a deep breath, squaring her shoulders. She was delighted to be included in Amanda's celebration, but was filled with mixed emotions at seeing Matt again. He hadn't called after the last time she'd seen him, and she couldn't help but wonder whether he had any feelings at all about her being here again this evening.

The heavy door opened, and Willie was relieved to see Craig standing there proudly in his dress uniform.

"Hi! I'm glad you could make it. Amanda will be thrilled." He took Willie's free hand and gave it a shake. "You know she's giving you all the credit for getting us married, even though you didn't actually conduct the ceremony."

Willie handed him the present and stepped into the entry as he thanked her. "I really don't deserve any credit." She swallowed a hysterical giggle. Matt must be ready to string her up by her hair. No wonder he hadn't called. Then she chided herself silently, *stop wondering how he feels about everything! It isn't important.*

"Do you remember my Aunt Violet?"

Craig's gaze lingered for only a second on Violet's pale blue hair, piled into a knot bisected by a set of ornate chopsticks inlaid with mother-of-pearl. Then he leaned forward to give her a kiss on the cheek. "How could I forget?" he asked with a smile. "Come and say hello to Mandy."

He led the way through the living room, stopping to set their present on a side table covered with other gifts and to hand them each a glass of champagne from a passing tray. Then he escorted them outside to a wide deck, where Amanda was talking to Matt and several other people. When she saw Willie she gave an excited whoop and hugged her, almost spilling Willie's champagne.

"You look radiant," Willie said to her, keeping her eyes on Amanda after one hasty glance at Matt. That quick peek had been long enough to register that the cream linen suit he was wearing did devastating things to his tanned skin and dark eyes. Willie ignored the rapid patter of her pulse as she concentrated on the young woman who stood before her, glowing with happiness.

"Thank you," Amanda said. "Craig gets the credit for that."

Her words sent a blush up her new husband's neck and across his lean cheeks. Willie found his embarrassment almost as endearing as the proprietary arm he slid around Amanda's waist.

"You look so pretty," Amanda continued, glancing at Willie's pale pink dress. "And you, too," she said to Violet. "We're so glad you could both be here. Aren't we, Matt?" She turned to her brother, who had been silent during the exchange.

Matt was watching Willie through narrowed eyes, as he sipped his drink. At his sister's words he nodded slowly, his gaze lingering on Willie's throat, making her swallow nervously. As her hand fluttered up to see if her pearls had become twisted, he turned to include Violet in his greeting.

"Of course we're glad to see you again," he said smoothly. "Welcome."

Amanda turned to make introductions. Willie paid strict attention to each new name and face, not daring to look at Matt.

He in turn was staring at her with single-minded concentration. He willed her to face him and meet his eyes, but Willie, looking as delicate as an angel in a dress that floated around her like a cloud, her red-gold hair waving away from her face and a row of pearls in each ear, was doing a damned good job of ignoring him.

Matt found that irritating. He was the one with the right to be annoyed, and he itched to tell her so. After all, Willie Webster, justice of the peace and purveyor of the romantic myth, had gotten exactly what she wanted.

Willie managed to turn her back on him completely as she edged away. Violet was at her elbow. Raking a hand through his dark hair, Matt decided to bide his time. He went inside, crossed the crowded living room and made his way into the spacious kitchen, stopping to talk to people as he went and eventually succeeding in drowning out the lilting sound of Willie's voice.

He had invited several co-workers from the law firm who had met Amanda before, as well as her friends from the library where she worked. For a shy girl she seemed to make friends easily. Everyone liked her.

Only a handful of Craig's crew mates had obtained liberty to be there, and no other family members from either side were present. Craig's were too far away, and Amanda had no close relatives except for Matt. Still, a respectable number of people had shown up for the last-minute party.

The burden of his responsibility as Amanda's only real family weighed heavily on Matt, he thought, as he replenished his glass and walked back outside to a more private corner of the deck. Then he remembered that now Craig would be considered her closest relative, not himself. He mumbled a curse and took a large swig of his drink.

Willie was standing on the other side of a wide post, but Matt didn't see her until it was too late to retreat without being rude.

"Hi," she said, barely glancing at him over her shoulder before returning her attention to the wide sweep of lawn and the shimmering blue water beyond.

Matt paused to study the way the sun turned her hair to fire, then joined her at the railing. He wondered what she was thinking. And he wondered even more why the urge to wrap his hands around her neck had been replaced by the even stronger need to bury his face in her scented hair. Another couple stood only a few feet away, so Matt did neither.

"No weddings today?" he asked her, instead, maintaining a discreet distance between them.

She looked up at him then, a mischievous twinkle in her eyes. "Even the merry matchmaker gets an occasional day off," she said, sipping her champagne.

Matt's gaze strayed to the drop of moisture that clung to her full bottom lip when she lowered the glass. Something tightened and threatened to snap deep inside him. Deliberately he ignored it.

"Well, I guess you've done all the harm you can to this family," he said in a low voice as he angled his back toward the other couple.

Willie's eyes blazed, and he could see her fingers tighten on the glass she held. Almost idly he wondered if she was about to dash it in his face. Animosity seemed the safest of the emotions she raised in him, and he smiled grimly in the face of her fury.

"How can you say that?" she gasped. "Amanda and Craig are so happy. Surely even you can't argue that."

"But how long will it last?" he questioned, gazing past her into the distance.

Willie found herself swallowing her anger as she heard the thread of pain in his voice. If only he could trust in the young couple's love for each other. Willie's heart softened, and her anger left her as quickly as it had come. She laid a gentle hand on Matt's sleeve, searching for the words to reach him.

"Give them time," she said finally, "and space."

"Are you implying that I would deliberately sabotage their marriage?" His eyes were glittering and his features had hardened as he glared at her.

Willie sighed, removing her hand when he stared at it pointedly. "No, not deliberately. But please don't let your own views influence them."

He shrugged before draining his glass. "I want Amanda's happiness more than anything," he said. "You believe that, don't you?"

Willie did her best to ignore the breathless response his earnest expression called up. "Of course. We want the same thing."

He thought about that for a moment. "Perhaps you're right," he said, though his tone was doubtful.

Suddenly his face relaxed, and his smile reminded Willie just how charming he could be when he wanted.

"Amanda's glad you came, and so am I," he said, his sudden mood change making Willie uneasy. "I hope that you and Violet will stay awhile."

Willie glanced at her watch. "I suppose we can."

Matt became the congenial host. "I have to make a toast in a few minutes. Then Craig and Amanda are going to cut the cake. There'll be dancing after that, if you'll save me one." His brown eyes held hers as he waited for her reply.

Willie threw caution to the wind. "Okay."

His smile widened briefly, making her wonder if she'd been wise to agree. Dancing with Matt promised to be a heady experience.

When he left her to greet some late arrivals, Willie wandered through the spacious house, looking for her aunt and thinking how foolish it was to allow herself the slightest feelings of attraction toward a man with Matt's cynical attitude. She would only be hurt if she weren't careful. Then she shrugged philosophically. Even a man as embittered as Matt could change if he really wanted to.

Willie eventually found Violet reading palms in a quiet corner of the game room. Two women who looked about Amanda's age were giggling and waiting their turn, plying Violet with questions as she studied the hand of a woman who had been introduced earlier as Amanda's boss at the library.

"I see you're keeping busy," Willie said as Violet bent over the librarian's palm.

"I wish I had my cards," Violet muttered, pushing her wire-framed glasses up on her nose. "They're much more reliable."

"Do you see any men there?" the librarian asked, leaning forward as Violet traced her lifeline with a finger. "I don't meet too many in my work, you know."

Willie squeezed Violet's shoulder. "Don't strain your eyes," she murmured, turning away as Violet spoke reassuringly to the other woman.

Willie had just finished a sampling of food from the plentiful buffet table when she saw two waiters carrying out a beautiful three-tiered cake covered with frosted doves and pink roses. They set it carefully on a round table next to where Amanda and Craig were standing, holding hands. For a small reception Matt had spared no expense.

Fresh champagne was circulated among the guests gathered in the huge living room as he stepped beside the newlyweds and held his glass high. Knowing how he felt about Amanda's marriage, Willie couldn't help but admire the classy way he carried out his duties.

When Matt had everyone's attention, he spoke out in a clear, deep voice. "Join with me in wishing our new bride and groom every happiness for a bright and blessed future."

He turned and looked at Amanda. "You know how much I love you, Mandy, as does everyone in this room. If you need anything, you have only to ask." His attention shifted to Craig, and Willie was close enough to see the sudden glint in Matt's dark eyes. "Take good care of my sister," he said, "or you'll have me to deal with."

Everyone chuckled at his words except Craig and Willie. They both knew how deadly serious Matt was. Willie realized again that Matt could be either a formidable enemy or a powerful friend. The sudden image of him as a lover was enough to make her feel heady with desire before she chased the fantasy from her mind.

After the toasts were given, Willie found her way to Matt's den, where she became absorbed in his law books. She had slipped off her shoes and was curled into a leather chair, reading through a familiar tome, when she became aware that she was no longer alone. When she looked up, Matt was standing in the doorway. He had shed his jacket and loosened his tie.

"You did a lovely job with this reception," Willie said, closing the heavy book. "And with the toast."

Matt's gaze met hers as his blunt fingers pushed back the strands of hair that feathered across his wide forehead. "I meant what I said. Did you think I would deliberately embarrass my sister?" he asked.

"No, of course not. I know how much you love her." Willie got up and slid her shoes back on, smoothing her skirt and replacing the book. "I hope you don't mind my being in here."

He stepped back as she brushed past him. "Of course not. You don't have to leave."

Willie could see that some of the guests were departing. Amanda and Craig were saying goodbye to a group at the front door.

"Nice of you to acknowledge that," she said in reply to Matt's remark. "I'm sure you consider my degree wasted." She couldn't understand why she always had the urge to bait him, to stir things up.

"Now that you mention it, I have wondered if you didn't miss practicing real law." There was curiosity on his face, and something more she couldn't read. She ignored the familiar tug of attraction.

"You mean practicing the kind of law you practice?" She couldn't resist the barb, then found herself regretting it almost immediately when his expression darkened.

"I'm sorry," she said quickly as he moved closer. "That wasn't nice."

"No, it wasn't," he agreed, pushing her back into the den before she could protest, shutting the door behind them and abruptly cutting off the party noises. His grin was ruthless, and Willie forgot to breathe. He looked dangerous and very masculine. She struggled to return his predatory smile with a cool one of her own.

The arrogant thrust of her chin and the chilly little tilt to the corners of her mouth were Matt's final downfall. Without allowing himself time to reconsider, he curled his fingers around her upper arm and pulled her slowly toward him. The way her eyes darkened from gray to green, and the shimmering gold band around the irises fascinated him as he stared down at her intently.

"What are you doing?" she asked.

The breathlessness of her voice gratified him. "What I should have done when you first walked in the door," he said. "I'm shutting you up."

Willie's lips parted in surprise, and he took full advantage. The moment his mouth touched hers, the urge to grind her tender flesh against her teeth subsided, and he found himself nibbling gently, instead, caressing her with the very tip of his tongue, determined to coax from her a response as heated as the one he had been cursed with ever since he'd first seen her. Beyond the animosity, beyond the annoyance she whipped up in him with her romantic notions, there lay only need, only hunger. He increased the pressure of his mouth and gathered her close against his hard body.

With a tremor of surrender she melted into him.

"Damn, you don't play fair," he said on a groan before he lowered his head again.

Willie was struggling to make sense of his comment, to hang on to some shred of control, when his lips left hers to glide across her cheek. With a shiver of pleasure she felt his tongue lightly touch the lobe of her ear, toying with one pearl stud, before he found his way to the tender flesh beneath the point of her jaw. Arching, Willie murmured her approval as he traced the sensitive cord down the side of her neck, his warm breath bathing her skin in its sensuous path. Holding the back of her head still, he buried his face in her hair.

"This is crazy," she whispered.

"I know." His voice was ragged.

She expected him to loosen his hold, to move away. Instead he turned his head, coming back to her mouth. The hands she had raised to ward him off slid harmlessly back around his neck, her fingers tangling in his heavy, straight hair. His arms surrounded her in a powerful embrace and his tongue plunged with heated insistence. Willie's knees weakened when she felt his fingers brush the side of her breast.

As her lips parted helplessly, a harsh groan worked its way up from his chest. His tongue coiled with hers and his hands stroked her from waist to hips in a fluid caress that brought her even closer.

The instant Willie felt his aroused body pressed against her she froze. Everything was going too fast— Matt's sudden attention, his puzzling comment, his stubborn stand on Amanda's marriage. Willie needed time to sort through the emotions that crowded her mind and were becoming more confusing by the minute. To concede that Matt was no knight in shining armor was an understatement. The question was, what were his intentions? And how did she feel?

Willie began to struggle.

Immediately Matt lifted his mouth, his arms dropping to his sides. His cheeks were flushed and his breathing was labored. Willie was still achingly aware of his taste on her mouth.

"I'm sorry," he said, stepping back. He looked slightly dazed.

"What did you mean?" she asked, her voice thin. "You said something before you . . ." Her words trailed off, and she gestured meaninglessly as she tried to remember what he had said. "You said I didn't play fair."

She was definitely confused by what had happened between them, but also exhilarated at the way he could turn her emotions upside down with a kiss, a seductive embrace, even a burning glance. The feelings he raised in her weren't gentle, as she'd imagined love to be—they were explosive. Clearly an attack of physical lust.

Hormones, as Matt had insisted before. Whatever it was, she found that she liked it. Or she had until she'd come up against the evidence of his response. Then she had panicked.

Resisting the urge to lick his taste from her lips, she waited for an answer to her question.

Matt ran a hand across his chin, blinking several times. "I'm not sure what I meant," he admitted finally. "You must think that I've completely flipped, dragging you in here, pouncing as I did."

Something in the way he refused to look at her, as if he were embarrassed by his own actions, opened some well of tenderness inside her.

"No," she said softly. "I don't think anything like that."

He raised his head and their eyes met. Gently he reached out a hand to touch her shoulder. "Are you okay?"

She couldn't resist the urge to tease him a little. "I can take care of myself, remember? If I had really wanted to stop you, I would have. Besides, nothing major happened."

For an instant something flashed across his face, then his expression smoothed out. "I guess I'm lucky I didn't end up on my back on the carpet again," he said wryly.

Willie eyed the cream linen of his slacks. "Would I do that?"

"Promise me you won't, and I'll kiss you again," he challenged, looking more like his old arrogant self.

With a light laugh she stepped away. "Something tells me that's a promise I wouldn't be wise to make," she replied.

Matt caught her hand in his. "We'd better go back to the party before someone starts wondering about the closed door and decides to investigate."

"Of course." She swallowed the niggle of disappointment that he hadn't pursued the subject, or her, further. "You have other guests."

"No one as interesting as you," he murmured, surprising her as he put a hand on the brass knob. Before he opened the door, he looked back over his shoulder. "I'll bet the dancing has started in the other room. And you promised me." He pushed open the door and held out his hand.

Willie wondered if going back into his arms so soon was a good idea. "Before we leave," she said quickly, "I really wish you'd stop worrying about Amanda. Why do you feel so strongly that her marriage is a mistake?"

"I'm not so blind that I can't recognize a lost cause," he said.

The bitter edge to his voice surprised her as his hand shifted to the pocket of his slacks.

"They're married and all I can do now is be here to pick up the pieces," he finished resignedly.

Willie studied the hardened planes of his face. "You really believe that," she said. "But why are you so certain this marriage will end in disaster?"

He stared down at her, brown eyes turned chilly. "Because they almost always do," he said quietly. "You only see the beginning, the hope and the ignorant happiness. I see the reality."

Willie shook her head, denying his words. "You're so wrong," she said.

Matt's jaw tightened. "If you saw what I see every day—"

"If *you* saw," she interrupted. "The kind of love I see doesn't sour, doesn't stop. It's not some rosy, romantic cloud that burns off in the daylight. It lasts. My marriages last."

He muttered a rude word.

"You see only the failures," she continued. "What about the people who never seek your services?"

For a moment he seemed to consider her arguments. Then he shook his head. "Come down to my office, and I'll show you."

"Okay," she said, surprising them both. "I will. As long as you agree to come to my weddings."

His brows arched as he studied her silently. Then he grinned, a grin without warmth, without humor. Willie wondered if she was making a huge mistake. No, something drove her on. Some small but growing certainty that deep within Matthew Bailey there was a tiny grain of hope, of love. Something that was worth nurturing. She just knew that he was capable of returning what she was beginning to feel for him, despite his prickly exterior and her own reservations.

"Come on," she coaxed, flashing him an impudent smile, knowing he couldn't resist a challenge. "What do you have to lose but a little cynicism?"

"Indeed," he said. "That's what I've been wondering myself. Let's make this interesting, then." He paused, considering. "You sit in on three of my cases, and I'll attend three of your weddings. We'll see whose opinion changes."

Willie was about to agree when a look of distaste crossed his face. "As long as the weddings are on the ground," he added. "No more parachuting from vintage airplanes."

"Agreed! And I'm sorry about that one. If you had told me you didn't like flying—"

"There's flying, then there's flying," he interrupted. "And I'm not sure that you and I agree on what qualifies as such. Now if you wanted to conduct a wedding underwater..."

It was Willie's turn to shudder with distaste. "That's quite all right. We'll keep them on the ground." She could think of one ceremony already that she didn't want him to miss. He was bound to change his mind about love after that.

Matt was pleased with the terms, confident that Willie would lose her air of naïveté once she had listened to some of the cases that came through his office. He didn't examine very closely his motives in wanting to disillusion her; he only knew that once he shattered her romantic notions, he would have more of a chance of getting what he wanted. And what he wanted was Willie. No romantic trappings, no meaningless promises or misplaced sentimentality. Just her sexy, delightful body wrapped around him for as long as it took to satisfy the hunger that clawed at his gut whenever they crossed swords.

"Now that we have that settled," he said in a husky voice, "how about that dance?"

She put her hand in his and he led her from the den, telling himself that for tonight holding her in his arms and moving to the soft music that flooded the house would be enough. Soon there would be more, much more, between them. He could wait.

"WHAT TIME is Mr. Bailey picking you up?" Aunt Violet asked Willie, lifting the lace curtain to stare out the front window.

"Anytime now." Willie plucked an imaginary speck of lint from the sleeve of her dark blue dress and picked up her purse and white gloves, recalling with a little shiver of reaction how romantic it had been dancing with Matt in the darkness of the nearly deserted deck. They had drifted together, not speaking, until he had had to excuse himself to say goodbye to some departing guests. Then Aunt Violet had appeared, and it had been time to leave.

Now Willie was looking forward to the wedding she would perform that afternoon, wearing a traditional robe over her tailored dress. Matt was going to pick her up and attend the ceremony as her guest.

Willie smiled to herself. Even his tough heart couldn't fail to be touched by the story behind this wedding, one it had taken fifty years and a healthy dose of either luck or fate to pull off.

At the sound of tires on gravel, Willie took a last look at herself in the hall mirror. "I'll see you later," she said to Violet, who was moving knickknacks around on the mantel.

"I still don't understand why he's going with you," Violet replied in a worried voice, "but it's nice that you're seeing each other again."

Willie was touched at the caring in her voice. "I already told you. He's going to attend three of my weddings."

"And you're going to sit in on three of his divorces." Violet sniffed, as if even speaking that last word offended her.

"I am a lawyer, remember."

Violet shook her head as the bell rang. "Just don't get hurt," she said. "Matthew is a complicated man."

Willie gave her a last pat before crossing to the front door. "Matt would never hurt me," she said with more confidence than she was feeling, before she turned the knob.

He looked terrific in the same three-piece suit he'd worn to the wedding in Issaquah. "All set?"

"Yes. I hope you are," she couldn't help but say.

Instantly the expression in his dark eyes grew wary. "No planes," he said.

"No planes." Her smile widened as he turned to say goodbye to Violet. Then he picked up Willie's briefcase from a chair in the entry, and took a garment bag from the halltree and followed her to his car.

"It's a beautiful day for a wedding," she said, looking up at the clear blue sky. "Too bad we aren't going to be outside."

"Planning an outdoor ceremony can be asking for trouble in this part of the country." Matt allowed his gaze to wander as he held open the car door, admiring the way her skirt skimmed over her slim hips.

"What's so significant about this wedding?" he asked, obviously curious. "I know you're not going to waste one of your three chances to change my mind on something ordinary."

She smiled up at him before he closed her door. "You'll see."

When the car drew up in front of a small building needing a paint job in one of the older sections of town, Matt glanced around curiously. "Is this it?"

"Yes. Let's go in." Willie waited impatiently while he circled the car and opened her door.

When they went inside Matt stopped again, looking around inquiringly. The main room, though shabby, had been decorated with loving care. A white runner covered the worn carpet, and several rows of folding chairs had been set up. Flowers and candles were grouped at the far end, where Willie and the bridal couple would stand. Streamers crisscrossed the ceiling.

There were a few people already there, but to Matt's surprise they were all elderly. Family, he decided. Willie took her briefcase, thanking him before approaching a silver-haired woman wearing a pink lace dress.

To Matt's further surprise, Willie introduced the woman as the matron of honor. Before he could pull Willie aside to ask what was going on, other people began to arrive, people of all ages. A little girl stopped to stare up at him, thumb in her mouth. A little boy in a suit with short pants announced in a shrill voice that he was going to be his grandma's ring bearer.

Matt turned puzzled eyes to Willie.

"This wedding has been waiting fifty years to take place," she explained in a low voice. "I'm honored to be the one to finally perform it."

"What do you mean? What's going on?" he asked, glancing around again.

Willie's gaze clouded as she looked up at him. "The bride and groom fell in love as teenagers. Then the bride's parents moved across the country, taking her with them. Times were hard, and she lost touch with the groom. Eventually they married other people."

Matt opened his mouth to comment, but Willie continued speaking softly.

"A few years ago, after they had both raised families and become widowed, a friend of the groom managed to track her down, and she wrote him a condolence letter. They began to correspond."

She dabbed at her eyes with a lace handkerchief and gave Matt a watery smile. He was surprised to realize how much he had been caught up in the story.

"Sorry," she said. "I just find it all so touching."

It was easy for him to see that she had hoped it would touch him, too. After all, that was the whole point of his presence. He managed to maintain an expression of polite interest; it would take more than a sentimental story of two lonely old people to change his mind about matrimonial bliss.

"The bride, Muriel Bird, came back to Seattle a month ago to visit the groom, Homer Spence." Willie hesitated, a slight frown crimping her pale brows, no doubt because of Matt's lack of reaction. "And here we are today," she concluded. "Isn't it funny how life turns out sometimes?"

Matt forced himself to remain untouched by sentiment. "It sure is," he agreed noncommittally.

If Willie was disappointed, she didn't show it. "I'll see you later," she said, patting his arm. "Find a seat anywhere."

She disappeared through a side door, carrying her garment bag, and Matt settled into a folding chair toward the back. While she was gone the room filled up with wedding guests. Conversation was hushed against a backdrop of piano music. Matt recognized one of the songs that his grandmother used to sing to him.

Willie swept back into the room in her long robe, her hair pinned up on top of her head, curly tendrils already pulling free. Matt felt an unexpected burst of pride at the elegant picture she made, standing calmly before them, her smile sweet and her hands folded.

When she gestured for the groom to join her at the front of the room, Matt almost smiled at the man's slow progress. By God, he had to hand it to the old guy. His gait might be shaky, but his shoulders were squared and there was a determined tilt to his chin as he turned to face the guests.

For a moment Matt envied him, before he realized that was exactly what Willie had intended. For him to be caught up in the sentimentality of the moment. Taking a deep breath, Matt turned his head as the wedding march burst forth.

When the ceremony was over, Willie and the bridal couple disappeared to sign the papers. Matt ignored the speculative gleam of a girl about Amanda's age and helped two other men rearrange the chairs for the reception.

"Have you sampled the punch and cookies yet?" Willie asked when she returned, sliding her arm through his.

He smiled down at the freckles dancing across her upturned nose. "No, I've been waiting to kiss the bride."

Her surprise was obvious, as was her delight. "Let me introduce you," she said, pulling on his arm.

After Matt had congratulated Homer and kissed Muriel on the cheek, he stepped back to watch Willie. She was honestly delighted at the couple's happiness, and treated them more as friends than customers. It was obvious her work made her happy. His clients might be relieved or elated at a victory, but they seldom made him feel the kind of warmth the new bride and groom were sharing with Willie as they thanked her.

For a moment Matt felt as popular as the local dogcatcher, before he reminded himself that his contribution was much more helpful in the long run than Willie's.

"If you're ready, I'll go change," she said to him, breaking into his thoughts.

"I'm ready," he said, dropping a kiss onto her soft mouth. He watched with fascination as color warmed her cheeks. His unexpected gesture had clearly flustered her.

"Well, then, I'll be right back," she murmured, turning away.

I'm more ready than you know, he thought as he watched her cross the room. *And much more determined.*

5

"I DIDN'T KNOW you had any weddings scheduled this morning," Violet said as she joined Willie in the small kitchen.

"I don't."

Violet eyed her niece's tailored blouse and skirt with curiosity. "Isn't that one of the outfits you used to wear when you worked at Pascoe and Hallquist?"

Willie set down her teacup and twirled around. "Do I look sufficiently lawyerlike?" she asked. She was sitting in on a case of Matt's that morning—not the right occasion to wear one of her flowing caftans.

"Willie," Violet began earnestly, "I'm not sure that I like what you're doing. I don't think it's a good idea."

Willie opened the refrigerator and got out the butter. "Matt and I have an agreement," she said, slicing bread for toast. "I'm prepared for the worst."

"This is a strange way to conduct a courtship," Violet muttered in a dire tone as she opened the blackberry jam.

"Who says it's a courtship?" Willie stuck her head back into the fridge, ignoring Violet's derisive snort.

She poured juice for them both and helped carry the food to the table. Before Violet could ask any more questions, Willie managed to divert her attention by reminding her she had promised two pies for the bake sale benefiting the local animal shelter.

AN HOUR LATER Willie was listening to Matt's opening arguments in a divorce hearing between a middle-aged wife and the husband who had left her for his young secretary. Matt was fighting for temporary support so the woman could attend vocational school. Willie watched him with growing respect as he questioned his client about her plans and the finances she would need to carry them out.

"Wouldn't you rather have a guaranteed income?" Matt asked her. "Going back to school and then finding a job when you haven't worked in over twenty years must be rather frightening."

The woman shook her head, chin high, and Willie was impressed with her determination and pride. "I want to start a new life," she said. "You were the one who suggested I go back to school, and it was a good idea. I'm not ready to sit at home and collect a check." Her gaze flicked over her ex-husband. "I have too much self-respect. With a little temporary help I can make it on my own. After all, I worked to put Bud through college."

Willie, who had heard the details of the case from Matt, had expected the woman to be defeated and bitter. Instead she seemed to be looking forward to new opportunities. When the judge awarded her the temporary support Matt had requested, Willie was pleased he had helped make it possible.

"Are you willing to admit yet that your romantic theories don't hold up in the real world?" he asked Willie over lunch. "You just saw a woman whose husband dumped her after a lifetime of devotion on her part. Where's the romance in that?"

Willie slid her hand across the table to cover his. "What I saw was a caring lawyer who was willing to fight for his client's best interests," she said. "And I'm proud of you."

Matt rolled his eyes and picked up the menu. "I think you missed the whole point," he said.

"Not at all," Willie replied, sipping her water. "I saw you in action and I was impressed." She didn't add just how impressed she had been, watching him pace back and forth before the bench like a restless lion, his long legs moving gracefully, his strong hands riveting her attention with each gesture. More than once she had lost the thread of the testimony, distracted by glimpses of raw male power beneath the civilized veneer. He was dominating and protective, and some primitive element buried deep within Willie couldn't help but respond.

Matt watched her nibble on her salad. He had hoped she would admit defeat after hearing his client's husband's testimony that he needed someone younger to make him feel alive. Hardly the words of a devoted husband. Matt had worse cases coming up; eventually Willie would realize her notions about marriage were unrealistic and outdated. The kind of love he had seen at the wedding she'd presided over was a fluke, something rare that, since the breakup of his own marriage to Michelle, Matt had become convinced wasn't meant for him.

He ordered coffee from the passing waiter.

"I'm sure you have something special in mind to drag me to next," he observed dryly, sipping the steaming liquid.

"Mmm," Willie murmured, a gleam in her eyes. "Could be."

"You don't have to be so mysterious. I'll be glad to tell you about my next case. It's a custody battle, little children torn apart by their parents' need for revenge. Very romantic."

Willie's eyes darkened with concern. "How sad. I hate it when the kids have to suffer, too."

"Meanwhile," he said, putting down his cup, "how about a walk by the pond before we both get back to work. I could use some sunshine and blue sky."

Willie had a wedding that afternoon, and he was booked solid with appointments. The strange reluctance he felt to return to his office surprised him. Usually he was eager for the work, often staying late in the evenings after everyone else had gone.

Most of the time he could immerse himself in a case and forget about the empty corners in his life, but lately he had trouble concentrating, and he blamed it entirely on Willie. He hadn't dated anyone else since he had taken that crazy plane ride, and he realized he didn't want to be with any other woman; but this obsession for Willie was driving him crazy. How could he expect his brain to function at full capacity when most of his blood supply seemed to have settled below his belt?

Willie smiled at his suggestion of a walk, tossing back her hair. Matt's body tightened uncomfortably as he stared at the shimmering waves.

"I wish I had something to feed the ducks," she said as they strolled outside into the sunshine.

Matt tucked her hand through the bend of his elbow. "Why don't you come over this evening. I'll barbecue, and we can watch the sailboats go by."

When Willie looked into his face his features seemed sharper, more intent, as he waited for her answer. It was the same watchful expression she had seen in the courtroom. Wanting to be with him, she refused his offer reluctantly. "I have a wedding out of town. I'll be back late," she said.

Beside her, Matt sighed. "Another time," he said. "Where's your wedding taking place?"

"On the ferry to Kingston. The reception's on the peninsula, then I have to catch a ferry back. I'd ask you to go along, but I don't know the people at all well."

"No matter. I always have paperwork to catch up on."

"You work too hard," she said. "I'll be willing to bet you take it home with you every night."

His eyes glittered. "You could change that," he murmured close to her ear. "Give me something else to keep my evenings busy." His voice dropped even lower. "And my nights."

Willie pulled away. Not sure how to answer, she said nothing and looked away to admire the petunias and marigolds blooming along the edge of the grass. After a few more minutes Matt glanced at his handsome gold watch and they turned back toward the parking garage.

"I'll call you," he said as he stopped by her car.

Willie looked up as his mouth descended on hers. His lips were warm, caressing. Long before she had had enough he pulled away. "Too bad about tonight," he murmured with a cocky grin as she began to unlock her door. She was halfway home before her pulse rate slowed to normal.

THAT EVENING Matt sorted through some papers as he waited for the steak on his gas grill to finish cooking. He had indeed brought work home to keep his mind off Willie, but her image kept getting in the way as he set aside a legal brief to put a potato into the microwave and pour himself another glass of wine. Then he gave up trying to concentrate on the dry legal phrases and opened the letter from Amanda he'd been saving to read with his dinner.

It was a relief to know that things were going well and she was happy. He had wondered, when he heard that Craig was leaving days after the reception on a training course, just how she would get along while he was gone.

Amanda was a sweet girl and he loved her dearly, but he knew she was used to things a certain way. She didn't adapt quickly to change and she was slow to make new friends. People liked her, but she was shy, unused to making the first move. And she hadn't found a job in Bremerton yet. She wrote that people were reluctant to hire service wives, assuming they would eventually be transferred. Reading between the lines, Matt sensed a certain restlessness. He picked up the phone and called her, suggesting she come home for a visit.

"I want to stay here," she said stubbornly. "But thank you for the offer."

Matt argued that Craig wouldn't mind if she came back while he was gone, but to no avail.

"I love you," Amanda said before they hung up, but Matt was still depressed as he cut into the steak. Even if she came home to visit, things wouldn't be the same. He remembered how jealous a younger Amanda had been when he'd married Michelle. The two females had disliked each other on sight and neither had changed her opinion through the three years the marriage had lasted.

Looking back, Matt could understand what a tough time his wife had had of it with a jealous preteen doing everything she could to cause trouble. That hadn't been the only problem, but it had certainly contributed to the breakup. Matt had sided with Amanda almost every time and had been totally blind to her manipulations. How insecure Amanda must have felt when he'd married, how afraid that he would stop loving her. As Matt buttered his baked potato, he wondered how much that had contributed to her shyness. And he realized that now it was his turn to be jealous. The thought was an uncomfortable one and he pushed it aside.

After their parents' accident Amanda had retreated behind a wall of solitude that Matt didn't seem to have the time or patience to penetrate. He had just started his law practice and was swamped with his first important case when she'd come to live with him. At the time summer camp had seemed like the ideal solution.

He had been relieved to know that Amanda had a special friend, but now, looking back, he knew he should have found more time for her himself. Never again would he be too busy when she needed him, he vowed silently as he stabbed a piece of steak with single-minded intent.

THE VERY NEXT WEEKEND Matt accompanied Willie to the second ceremony she had chosen for him to witness—a triple wedding uniting a young couple and giving the bride's parents and grandparents a chance to renew their vows. The older couples shared the same anniversary and had decided to renew their vows on the day of the young people's wedding. Soon all three couples would share the same anniversary date.

Willie hadn't enlightened Matt ahead of time. Sitting on the side aisle, he didn't pay much attention to the three men waiting at the front of the hall with Willie. He had glanced at the bride when she came down the aisle, only to have his attention brought back around as the wedding march started over again twice.

As the three couples stood before Willie, in her melodious voice, she explained the circumstances. Matt knew she expected him to be impressed by the long marriages of the two older couples and the love that was still plain to see on their lined faces. Despite himself he was impressed. Not that he would admit it for a second.

"WHAT DID YOU THINK?" Willie asked when she joined him after the lengthy ceremony to go to the reception that was being held at a private country club.

"Very nice," he said, studying her petite figure in the royal blue caftan. "A little loose for my taste, though."

"Not me," Willie exclaimed, laughing. "I meant the wedding—what did you think of the wedding?"

"What if you had gotten mixed up and married the wrong spouses?" he teased, watching her face and fighting down the urge to place his lips on the spray of freckles that danced across the bridge of her nose. "Would they have to switch all around?"

"You silly. They were already married, except for Jennifer and Brad. Besides, I never mix up my couples. I've done double weddings before and kept the people straight."

He sighed in mock relief. "You don't know how glad I am to hear that."

He stopped by his car as she slapped at him playfully with her clutch purse. "Some romantic you are," she teased.

Matt immediately put his arms around her and pulled her close, oblivious of the other guests going to their cars. "I warned you," he murmured, enjoying the feel of her slight body pressed to his. "But just because I'm not romantic, don't think for a minute that I don't want you, because I do." He rubbed his lower body against hers for emphasis.

This time Willie didn't panic as she pulled out of his arms. She glanced around, but no one was paying any attention. "We'd better go," she said reluctantly, ignoring the sudden heat that flooded her cheeks.

The room where the reception was being held had been redecorated to resemble a fairyland. Bare branches painted white had been strung with tiny blue twinkle lights to match the colors of the wedding party and placed in pots all around the room. The band was already playing and couples drifted to the dance floor after they went through the receiving line.

Matt stood beside Willie as she spoke briefly to each of the three newly married couples, and was impressed by the effortless way she made them all feel special. He admired the unique gift she had for turning an acquaintance into a friend.

After she had introduced him to the bride's grandparents and they had moved down the rest of the line, he cupped her elbow and leaned forward. "Do you want to get something to eat?" he asked, "or shall we take advantage of the music and dance first?"

"That's an easy question to answer," she murmured, sliding one arm around his neck. The spicy scent of his cologne filled her nostrils and the heat of his body warmed her, making her relax against him. Matt was by far the best-looking male at the reception, she thought proudly.

He curved his arms around her and began to move slowly to the music. His lead was sure and strong; Willie followed him effortlessly. After looking around the large room, she smiled up at him.

"They've spared no expense," she said.

His gaze upon her upturned face was intent. "How long do we have to stay?" he asked.

"Long enough to be polite."

"I don't feel very polite right now." His voice had deepened to a possessive growl.

A shiver of nerves went through her. He was making no attempt to disguise what he wanted. He wanted her. For a moment panic made her stumble against him. Then she relaxed. This was Matt, the man she was coming to care for more each time she was with him. He might think he was cold and ruthless, but she knew better. He had qualities she admired; all she had to do was to persuade him to see that—and to convince him to have faith in the love she believed in wholeheartedly.

"One more dance," she said. "Then we'd better eat. I missed lunch."

His brows rose in question. "Why did you do that? You're too slender to be missing meals on purpose."

"I had a consultation. It ran late and I didn't have time to stop before my next appointment. I'm sure it happens to you, too."

"Of course it does," he admitted. "But that's different."

Willie bristled instantly. "Because your work is so much more important?" she asked sweetly.

"No, my beautiful little feminist. Because I can afford to miss a meal. You can't." He tapped her upturned nose with his finger for emphasis.

"Oh," she said softly, properly mollified. She ran her hand across his broad shoulder. "You must work out," she said.

He shrugged. "A little tennis, a little racquetball. Sometimes I swim. What about you?"

She smiled and shook her head. "I guess rushing from wedding to wedding keeps me in shape. Sometimes I run, but not nearly as often as I'd like to."

"Come and run with me in the mornings," he said. "Better yet, stay over."

Willie shivered at the possessive note in his voice. It was becoming more and more difficult to hide her growing feelings for him. "I'll think about it," she finally managed.

His confident smile dragged up a reaction from deep within her. "You do that."

The young bride and groom moved onto the floor, and everyone else stepped back to watch their first dance. After a moment the two older couples joined them.

"Let's get something to eat," Matt suggested. After choosing a selection from the buffet, they found an unoccupied table. Several people approached Willie to comment on the ceremony, and on each occasion she introduced Matt, subjecting him to an array of curious glances. Willie wondered what he would say if someone asked him what he did for a living, but luckily no one did.

After they had eaten and had a glass of champagne, Willie eyed the crowded dance floor. "Want to try it again?" she asked Matt, who had been staring at her for several moments.

"No, thanks. How about a nightcap at my house, instead?"

The silence stretched between them while Willie pondered his offer. She knew what he was really asking, and her body responded with a flood of awareness.

Willie tried to answer, but something was blocking her throat. Without looking at him, she nodded her assent and slipped her hand into his. If Matt wanted her, then she wanted to be with him, too. It was enough for now that he desired her, but she had to keep believing that love would follow.

"I DON'T KNOW what I'm doing here." Willie sat down nervously on one of the matching leather couches and smoothed her skirt over her shaky knees. She had changed from the flowing royal blue caftan into a simple shirtwaist dress after the wedding reception, but now she almost wished that she were still camouflaged within the enveloping folds of the other garment.

When she had agreed to come home with Matt for a nightcap, she had been very certain what she wanted. Now regrets started creeping in on her as he hung her coat in the hall closet and returned to the living room, his large frame filling the doorway.

"Liar," he accused softly as he crossed to where she sat primly on the edge of the cushion. "You know exactly why you're here."

Willie was at a distinct disadvantage as she craned her head back and returned his mocking gaze. Before she could protest, Matt's big hands reached down to cup her elbows and scoop her up to stand before him. He was so close that her breasts brushed the front of his jacket.

His dark eyes glinted with challenge even as his wide mouth curved into a tempting smile. "Let's get this over with." His voice was deep, compelling, and the scent of his cologne, something dark and dangerous, swirled around Willie as she fought to make sense out of his startling suggestion.

"What do you mean?" she squeaked as his hands slid to her hips and he dragged her closer.

"You've been wondering since we go into my car just when I was going to kiss you. Once I do, perhaps you can relax."

Before Willie could respond to his outrageous suggestion, Matt bent his dark head and captured her mouth with his own. She stiffened as he folded her into his masculine embrace, but the gentleness of his kiss disarmed her.

Tenderly Matt caressed her lips with his, and only when she yielded, returning the kiss, did he finally deepen it. The bold intrusion of his tongue swept away her defenses and made her heart flutter. When he finally lifted his head, she moaned a protest.

"See," he said in a husky voice. "It wasn't as bad as you thought it would be."

"Oh, no," Willie contradicted, raising her face for another kiss. "It was much worse."

Flashing a smile brimming with devilish charm, Matt bent to kiss her again. This time he made no attempt to leash his passion, and his mouth covered hers insistently, consuming her with fiery heat. Inhibitions fled as Willie returned the onslaught with controlled enthusiasm, tangling her tongue with his, stroking its rough-smooth textures as her hands kneaded the hard muscles of his shoulders.

Matt pulled away from her enticing mouth to release the top button of her dress with fingers that weren't quite steady. Willie trembled wildly as he brushed aside her collar and touched his tongue to the rapid pulse at the side of her throat. Willie's scent and the taste of her skin were driving him mad, shattering the control he prided himself on always maintaining.

He looked into the deep green of her eyes and saw his own desire reflected there. "You're so beautiful," he murmured, slipping loose two more buttons. He lowered his head to plant a kiss against the lightly freckled swell above the blue lace covering one small, perfect breast. How had he ever thought that bigger was better?

Willie's questing fingers caressed his nape, his ears, then explored the rigid line of Matt's jaw as he steeled himself to go slowly. One of his large hands lifted her breast within its lacy cup as he scraped his tongue across the hardened nipple pressing against the sheer fabric.

Willie arched closer to his ardent mouth as her hands clutched at his shoulders. He teased her with another stroke before releasing her long enough to yank his tie free and shrug out of his jacket. After one futile attempt at pulling the tail of his shirt loose, Willie's busy fingers went to its buttons. Matt caught her hand and kissed the knuckles before stripping off his shirt himself. Then he unbuttoned Willie's dress to the waist, pushing it from her shoulders and down her arms until it draped around her hips.

The wide, powerful expanse of Matt's bared chest fascinated Willie as she smoothed her fingers across the flat muscles and heated skin, sifting them through the broad patch of dense curls. As he held her in a loose embrace, she brushed her palm across one flat nipple, tensing when he hissed in a sharp breath.

"Did that hurt?" she asked.

He managed a wry chuckle as his hands reached around behind her. "It aches in a very sweet way. Let me show you."

He released the catch of her bra and slipped it away, staring at the feminine curves that were revealed.

"You're so beautiful," he whispered again, cupping her breast. It was creamy white against the tan of his hand. He trailed his thumb across the sensitive tip as Willie's breath caught.

"Perfect." He dipped his head and circled a pink bud with his tongue. A shudder ripped through her and she clutched at his upper arms.

"Hurt?" he asked, smiling down into her wide eyes.

"N-no." Willie wished he would continue what he had been doing. Her fingers inched into his thick, silky hair, urging his head back down. Against his big body she felt like a delicate doll.

Matt's hand eased over one rounded breast, his fingers stroking the nipple again, while his lips returned to the other. Their gentle tugging echoed deep within her, sending shivers of reaction all through her body. When he drew her deeper into his mouth, scraping ever so carefully with his teeth, she thought she would faint from the sheer ecstasy of it.

As if sensing her sudden weakness, he bent and scooped her high into his arms. He stood still, cradling her against his wide chest, until she opened her eyes and looked full into his face. How had she ever thought that brown eyes could be cold? His blazed with passion.

"I want you," he said, giving her time to retreat.

She managed a shaky smile. Willie was sure that what she felt for Matt was more than mere physical desire. In time he, too, would realize that the attraction between them was too strong to be only a fleeting hunger, easily satisfied. What they had was special, and rare. Meanwhile she could no more deny his fiery need than she could her own.

"I want you, too." Her voice was a bare whisper.

Hesitating no longer, he climbed the carpeted stairs, holding her close to his thundering heart, as she placed a kiss on the slightly whiskery skin of his jaw.

He shouldered open the door to a huge bedroom, but didn't give her time to look around before setting her on the wide bed and lying down near her. The bodice of her dress bunched under her uncomfortably and she sat up to finish taking it off.

Matt watched while she unbuckled the belt and slid the garment down over her hips. His gaze traveled possessively over her scantily clad body.

"Pretty," he said, glancing at the light blue half-slip trimmed with a wide border of lace.

Willie colored at his ardent inspection but opened her arms willingly as he moved back up the bed to gather her into his potent embrace.

"You're so strong," she said wonderingly as she caressed the heavy muscles of his shoulders. "No one would guess you sit behind a desk all day."

"Sometimes I don't." His hands hooked into the waistline of her silk half-slip, pulling her panty hose down with it. "No one would guess that you climb mountains and jump out of airplanes, either." His fingers encircled her slim ankle, and his light touch caused an instant reaction. "You seem too delicate." His lips feathered across her kneecap.

"Don't forget that I know karate," she gasped, remembering the time she had flipped him onto his back on the floor.

His hands skimmed back up her body, over the scrap of her panties, making her tremble in response, before he buried a chuckle between her breasts. "Don't think I haven't recalled your expertise every time I've thought about kissing you."

His hands and lips began to play across her sensitive flesh, driving any further thoughts of conversation right out of her head.

"Am I safe with you now?" he asked, trailing his fingers back across the silk of her panties.

Willie moaned, wishing he would remove that final barrier. Her fingers went to the buckle of his belt, and

Matt's stomach muscles quivered as he waited tensely until she released it. Rising from the bed with an impatient growl, he stripped off the rest of his clothes.

Willie's gaze swept over his big body as he stood unself-consciously before her. She'd always found him a little intimidating; now his brazen male strength made her feel secure, and very, very feminine. His darkened eyes were narrowed and his face was flushed with passion.

"What about you?" he asked softly. "Are you safe, or shall I protect you?"

Willie shook her head. "It's taken care of," she said, appreciating his concern. She had been on the pill for a while now.

This time when Matt came to her his touch was rougher, less controlled, the stroke of his hands more ardent, his mouth hotter. Willie returned his caresses, responding to his hunger.

When he swept aside her last remaining garment and wedged a solid thigh between her legs, she arched upward, her hands attempting to pull him even closer.

His palm slid down her belly as his fingers toyed with the edge of her fiery curls. Willie moaned helplessly, tossing her head from side to side. Mindless, molten desire had replaced reason.

Matt's touch became more intimate as his breathing turned ragged. "Do you want me as much as I want you?" he demanded, placing a kiss on her open lips.

Unable to form an articulate answer, vaguely aware that she had wanted something more from him, Willie grabbed his hand and pressed it against herself. In answer, Matt's fingers stroked her lightly, and she shuddered.

Positioning himself above her, he made them one with a long, sure stroke. For a moment he lay still, sheathed deep within her, as Willie wrapped herself around him. Then he began a rhythm that commanded a response from her very soul. The earth fell away and Willie soared, dimly aware of his voice rasping out her name as he followed her into oblivion.

Moments after, as Willie's breathing steadied and the tremors stopped, Matt shifted to her side and gathered her into his arms. She tucked her head onto his wide shoulder, her ear pressed to his chest. As she allowed her fingers to stroke idly down his arm, the rapid pounding of his heart gradually slowed to a steady beat. Willie's own pulse had also quieted, and her sated body melted against him.

"You're wonderful," he said, his breath stirring her hair. His hand traced long, soothing sweeps down the curve of her spine and the fingers of his other hand linked with hers. "Wonderful," he murmured again, his voice deepening as his breathing became slower and more regular.

Beside him, Willie's eyes drifted shut and she floated away.

SOMETIME LATER Matt padded silently out of the adjoining bathroom to stare tenderly down at Willie's sleeping form, tangled in the sheets, her lips swollen and her hair spread across the pillow like a red-gold halo. His body stirred in response to her abandoned pose, one pink-and-white breast saucily uncovered, and he frowned, jamming his hands into the pockets of the slacks he'd put back on.

He had thought that taking Willie to his bed would trim the edge from the hunger that had plagued him almost since the moment they had met; instead his appetite had grown. He wanted her again.

When her eyelids fluttered open and she stretched charmingly, his frown deepened.

"What time is it?" she asked, blinking and covering a yawn with one slim hand.

"Time to take you home." He needed some space to sort out his feelings. Things were getting too complicated. The idea of a short affair was a hell of a lot less appealing than it had been a few hours earlier, and that realization was enough to send him scrambling for cover.

Willie studied his closed expression, pulling the sheet up automatically.

"Kicking me out?" she asked in what she meant to be a light tone.

"Won't Aunt Violet wonder where you are?"

Oh, Lord. She hadn't given a thought to the woman. Aunt Violet would be worried sick since Willie had failed to come home after the wedding at the country club. She had mentioned the reception, but it must be the middle of the night by now. Her concern brushed aside any puzzlement over Matt's withdrawn expression.

"Could I use your phone?" She glanced around the spacious bedroom, coloring when she saw her dress laid neatly on the chair and her panty hose and slip on the floor beside the bed; her bra was nowhere in sight.

"It's right behind you on the headboard," Matt said in reply to her question.

Willie turned, holding the sheet carefully against her, and punched in her number. The phone rang several times before Aunt Violet answered in a sleepy voice.

"It's me," Willie said. "Sorry to wake you, but I didn't want you to worry."

Aunt Violet snorted. "Worry? Willie, girl, I knew you'd be with Matt. I read the cards before I turned in. Thanks for calling, though. Now can I get back to sleep?"

6

WRAPPING THE SHEET around herself, Willie scooped up her clothes and brushed past Matt on her way to the bathroom.

"I'll be dressed in a minute," she said, not quite meeting his eyes. Her gaze skimmed over his wide chest, then skittered downward. Realizing that was a mistake, she clutched her bundle of clothes tighter, almost dropping the sheet, and slammed the bathroom door harder than she'd intended.

When she came back out she saw Matt had taken the opportunity to finish dressing, too. He'd pulled a knit shirt over his head and slipped moccasins onto his feet.

For a moment their eyes met and held across the tangle of the unmade bed. Willie felt the hot color spreading over her cheeks as she noticed Matt's withdrawn expression.

"I hope I didn't take too long," she said, annoyed at his attitude. Perhaps the earth hadn't moved for him, or maybe it did every time he took a woman to bed and what he and Willie had shared there wasn't anything special to him. Still, he needn't act as though he couldn't wait to get rid of her.

"No," he said after a pause. "You didn't take too long."

"I could call a cab," she felt compelled to offer.

Her words must have conveyed some of what she was feeling. Matt's thick brows rose in surprise, and then he quickly crossed the room to take her into her arms.

"You must think I'm a prize jerk," he said, his voice low. "Of course I'll take you home." He planted a kiss on the tip of her nose before releasing her and clearing his throat. "Willie," he began, "tonight meant a lot to me. I hope you believe that."

She searched his face, then nodded. "Me, too."

He seemed to relax. "Good. Come on, it's late." He slipped an arm around her shoulders, keeping it there until they reached the front door which he stopped to lock behind them.

The night was mild, the sky full of stars. Willie glanced up at them as she followed Matt to his car, saw one shoot across the inky backdrop and made a quick wish.

"Pretty, aren't they?" he asked, pulling her attention back to him.

Willie gave a guilty start, then realized he had no idea what she'd been doing. She doubted he had ever wished on a star in his life. "Yes," she said briefly, sliding into the front seat. "Thank you."

When Matt eventually pulled into the small parking lot in front of the wedding chapel, he glanced at the front porch. "Violet left the light on for you."

"I hope she went back to sleep," Willie muttered as he followed her quietly up the steps. The last thing she wanted right now was a cozy talk with her aunt.

She paused at the door, not sure what to do. Matt tucked a finger under her chin and tilted her head up, bending close.

WOW!

THE MOST GENEROUS
FREE OFFER EVER!
From the Harlequin Reader Service

GET 4 FREE BOOKS WORTH $10.60

Affix peel-off stickers to reply card

4 FOUR FREE BOOKS 4

4 FOUR FREE BOOKS 4

PLUS A FREE ACRYLIC CLOCK/ CALENDAR

AND A FREE MYSTERY GIFT!

NO COST! NO OBLIGATION TO BUY!
NO PURCHASE NECESSARY!

Because you're a reader of Harlequin romances, the publishers would like you to accept four brand-new Harlequin Temptation® novels, with their compliments. Accepting this offer places you under no obligation to purchase any books, ever!

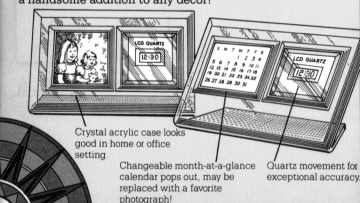

HARLEQUIN TEMPTATION® NOVELS

FREE!

 Harlequin Reader Service®

```
AFFIX
FOUR FREE BOOKS
STICKER HERE
```

YES, send me my free books and gifts as explained on the opposite page. I have affixed my "free books" sticker above and my two "free gift" stickers below. I understand that accepting these books and gifts places me under no obligation ever to buy any books; I may cancel at any time, for any reason, and the free books and gifts will be mine to keep!   142 CIH MDVS

NAME _____

                              (PLEASE PRINT)

ADDRESS _____ APT. _____

CITY _____

STATE _____ ZIP _____

Offer limited to one per household and not valid to current
Harlequin Temptation subscribers. All orders subject to approval.

```
AFFIX FREE
CLOCK/CALENDAR
STICKER HERE
```

```
AFFIX FREE
MYSTERY GIFT
STICKER HERE
```

WE EVEN PROVIDE FREE POSTAGE!

It costs you *nothing* to send for your free books — we've paid the postage on the attached reply card. And we'll pick up the postage on your shipment of free books and gifts, and also on any subsequent shipments of books, should you choose to become a subscriber. Unlike many book clubs, we charge *nothing* for postage and handling!

"You're really something," he said, "full of surprises." Beneath the porch light his eyes looked shadowed, their expression hidden. He kissed Willie softly, lingeringly, his hand caressing her cheek.

Without conscious consent, she responded, her lips clinging to his, her heart pounding in her chest. When he pulled away, she sighed.

"I'll call you," he said before he turned and left.

Willie stood and watched his car until it was out of sight. Touching her tender lips with the tip of her tongue, she let herself in and turned off the outside light. After she had put on her nightgown and robe, she sat in the bentwood rocker a long time before she finally went to bed. Her mind was full of images from earlier in the evening, but the moment her head touched the pillow she went to sleep, a smile on her lips.

THE NEXT MORNING, to Willie's surprise, Aunt Violet greeted her as if nothing unusual had happened. The questions Willie had braced herself for never came. Instead Violet asked her about her wedding schedule for the day and mentioned two appointments she herself had to read palms. If Willie's expression grew wary every time Violet began to speak, the older woman didn't seem to notice. By the time she left the kitchen, Willie was almost ready to volunteer the information Violet had refrained from requesting, just to get the strain of waiting over with.

"I'm going to the market down the street," Violet said, returning from her room with her handbag. "Need anything?"

"How about a sex—, I mean a six-pack of diet soda?" Willie suggested, coloring deeply at her slip.

Violet didn't even blink. "Good idea."

As soon as she left, Willie ran a hand through her hair and groaned. *Get a grip on yourself*, she chided. *People do it all the time. No one thinks anything about it. Be cool. It's no big deal.* So why did she feel as if she were wearing a red *A* on her forehead? She got up and paced to the mirror, anxiously scanning the image of her face.

Except for the little pink in her cheeks and a slight puffiness to her lower lip, she looked the same as she always had. No one could tell just by seeing you, she reassured herself. Then she looked into her own eyes more closely. There was a gleam there she'd never seen before. She couldn't help but smile at her reflection.

Without thinking, she grabbed the phone book, intent on calling Matt's office to wish him good morning. Then she remembered the way he had acted the night before after they'd made love. She put the directory back down. Better to let him have a little time to adjust to what was happening to them. He might fight it for a while, but Willie was confident that sooner or later he would see that they were meant to be together. He just had to!

Down at his office, Matt reached for the phone to call Willie, hesitated and pulled his hand back. She might still be asleep. She might be gone. He had no wish to get Aunt Violet, instead. What would he say if she asked him what his intentions were? She knew what he and Willie had been doing the night before. Would a woman of Violet's generation expect Matt to make an honest woman of Willie now?

He could no more tell her what his intentions were than he could tell himself. The truth was that his thoughts had been running in circles since he'd taken Willie home. He hadn't slept and now he was tired. Tired and confused. What had been meant as a simple seduction was getting very complicated.

His wandering attention focused on the way Willie had responded to him the night before, and his body tightened instantly. Matt lunged to his feet, intent on getting away from the suddenly stuffy office in which he'd been cooped up since five that morning.

When his secretary burst through the door, he swore under his breath and whipped his restless body around to stare out the window.

"What is it?" he barked over his shoulder.

Connie was used to his moods. "Mr. Peters is on the phone. He insists on seeing you tomorrow. Says he wants to go ahead with the divorce from that young woman he married last year, and he's demanding to know what the investigation turned up."

Matt groaned and raked a hand through his hair. "Poor bastard," he said without thinking. "I wanted him to let me draw up a premarital agreement, but he wouldn't listen."

"I told him you were booked solid, but he said you'd work him in."

Matt shook his head. "Some people never learn," he muttered. Mr. Peters was turning into a steady customer, one who didn't learn from past mistakes. Matt went to the file cabinet and took out a manilla envelope full of black-and-white photographs.

"Yeah," he said, looking up at Connie. "Schedule him after my last appointment, and tell him to bring his wife along. I think she'll want to see these, too."

Sometimes he really hated his job.

WILLIE LISTENED QUIETLY while Matt showed Mrs. Peters and her attorney some pictures taken by a private detective.

"I believe the man in the photos is your aerobics instructor," Matt said.

Willie almost pitied the woman, an attractive but somewhat hard-looking blonde, as her face paled. She was clearly shocked to have been found out. She glanced at one or two of the photographs before thrusting the whole bunch back at Matt.

After a pause that Matt deliberately let stretch a beat too long, he cleared his throat and named what Willie thought a generous settlement offer.

Mrs. Peters half rose from her chair. "We'll need a lot more than that to open our gym," she exclaimed.

Her attorney looked as if he would like nothing more than to gag her with the expensive silk scarf she wore around her neck. Grabbing her arm, he pulled her back into her chair.

"Shut up, Candy," he snapped before turning to Matt. "I need to consult with my client."

When Willie, Matt and Mr. Peters returned to the office a few moments later, the opposing counsel looked grim and Candy Peters subdued except for angry red flags across her thin cheeks.

"We accept your offer," he said, reaching to shake Matt's hand.

Mrs. Peters left the room without a backward glance. Her husband, a much older man, stopped to shake Matt's hand, but he didn't look happy. No reason for him to be.

Willie hoped his wife realized she was lucky to get what she did. Some women didn't deserve a good man.

"Still believe in the power of love?" Matt asked, shutting the door after the others had left.

"Of course I do," Willie responded. "This case proves nothing. It doesn't even apply."

Matt frowned, obviously puzzled. "Why not?"

"Because it had nothing to do with love," she explained as if he were a somewhat slow child. "He married her to recapture his youth, and she obviously married him for his money. You can't expect me to blame love for the fiasco we just witnessed."

Matt began to grin as he moved toward her. "No, I suppose that would be too much to expect. I give up," he murmured, drawing her into his arms. "At least for now. I can't think about logical arguments when I'm around you. All I can think about is this." He lowered his head, covering her mouth with his.

Willie responded as she always did, returning his kiss with the passion his touch ignited in her. For a long moment they stood wrapped in each other's arms, and when Matt finally broke away they were both breathing hard.

"Let's go to my house," he suggested, eyes dark with desire.

"I can't," Willie moaned with genuine regret. "I have two weddings back at the chapel."

"When will you be finished?"

"Too late. There's a wedding in Bellingham first thing in the morning."

He frowned but didn't argue. "Dinner tomorrow night then? Wear something special and we'll go downtown to that new club on the waterfront."

Willie reached up to push back the lock of hair that had fallen across his forehead, giving him a rakish appearance. "That sounds lovely," she said. "I'll be through early, so I'll have plenty of time to get ready."

Matt dropped one more kiss on her lips before letting her go. Willie felt a twinge of regret at what she was missing that evening as she walked down the hall from his office, but she had the next night to look forward to, after all. And she still had to think about one last wedding to sway Matt over to her way of considering marriage and love.

Back in his office, Matt decided to stop by his health club on his way home. He'd been neglecting his workouts lately; perhaps that was why he felt restless and out of sorts. Even his work wasn't as satisfying as usual.

Connie came in as he was clearing off his desk.

"I'm out of here," she said, pushing back her straight blond hair with one hand.

Matt looked up and smiled. Connie was a good secretary. He had been attracted to her when she'd first come to work for him but had resisted doing anything about it. He didn't believe in complicating things at the office.

Connie had made it clear on more than one occasion that she would welcome his attention, but he always pretended not to notice.

She came closer, and the scent of her expensive cologne teased his nostrils. It was heavy, not like the floral fragrance Willie favored. He almost sneezed.

"Big plans for the evening?" she asked, raising one perfect eyebrow.

Matt opened a file drawer and pulled out a thick folder. "'Fraid so," he said with a smile. "You know I always take work home."

Connie reached out coral-tipped fingers to straighten his tie as they faced each other across the desk. Her full lips puckered into a pout. "You know what they say about all work," she teased, dropping her hand reluctantly. "I could stay for a while and help you with it here."

Matt stepped back and slammed the drawer. "I appreciate that," he said, making a note to give Connie a raise and to keep more distance between them. A confrontation would only cause her to quit in embarrassment, and she was a damned good secretary. "But I need to get home."

He stepped around her to the door, pausing there. "If you're ready, I'll walk you out."

With a shrug and a good-natured smile, Connie strolled past him. "Can't blame a girl for trying," she said lightly.

WHEN WILLIE GOT HOME to the wedding chapel there was a long letter from Amanda waiting for her. Kicking off her shoes, Willie began to read it while her dinner of leftover spaghetti was reheating.

Amanda sounded lonely. It seemed she hadn't made any friends yet, even though she wrote that a couple of the other wives had invited her over when she and Craig had first moved in.

Willie sighed, remembering how withdrawn Amanda could be in a new situation. It had taken her weeks at summer camp to become comfortable with the other kids, and by that time some of them had already decided she was a stuck-up snob. Willie had had a discreet talk with the most popular girls to smooth the situation over.

Now it sounded as though Amanda were doing the same thing again, mooning over Craig instead of getting out and making friends to keep her company while he was at sea.

Amanda didn't come right out and say she was lonesome, but it was there between the lines. She said how happy Craig made her and how she didn't need anyone else, but she had already told Willie he had a six-month cruise coming up in the very near future. What would she do then?

Willie wondered if Matt had picked up on Amanda's unhappiness, or if his sister had presented a cheerier front to him. She would have to ask him the next evening at dinner.

Violet came in as Willie was dishing up the spaghetti. "Hi," Willie greeted her, her gaze flickering over Aunt Violet's lavender hair. Compared to some of the colors she used, it looked almost normal. "Want some spaghetti? There's plenty."

"Sure. I've been down at the senior center doing fortunes and manicures, and I'm starved." She spent a couple of afternoons a week there, helping out and entertaining the old people. "They wanted to know when you'd be in again," she said, pouring herself a cup of tea.

Willie went whenever she could to visit and to read aloud to those who could no longer read themselves. "I'll have to check my schedule."

"You don't have a wedding tomorrow night," Violet said. "Come to bingo with me."

Willie felt her face go warm. "I can't. I have a date."

Violet carried their plates to the table. "With Matthew Bailey?"

"Yes," Willie said reluctantly, hoping Violet wouldn't comment about the other evening.

She didn't, saying only, "I hope he's taking you someplace nice."

When Willie named the club, a new place on one of the piers at the foot of the downtown area, Violet's eyes widened. "I knew that boy had class," she said with a smug grin.

Before she could say more, Willie thought it wise to change the subject.

THE NEXT EVENING Matt found himself suddenly dissatisfied with everything; from the knot in his tie to the way his hair lay over his ears. Even the jacket to his favorite suit didn't seem to fit quite as well as he'd remembered. He finally glanced at his watch, gave his hair a final swipe and refrained from redoing his tie one last time.

Slamming the front door behind him, he thought grimly that he wouldn't be surprised if the car had a flat tire or refused to start. It had been a rotten day and now he was annoyed at himself for being as nervous as a kid on his first date.

He wanted everything to go perfectly this evening. And he wanted it to end with Willie naked in his arms, as passionately responsive as she had been the other night. Already it seemed ages since he'd held her, kissed her, looked into her twinkling gray-green eyes. At least the car started without incident, and in a moment he was traveling down the main road.

The one bright spot of his day so far had been another letter from Amanda, filled with lighthearted chatter about married life. He discovered he didn't mind a bit that so far his dire predictions were not coming true; he wanted her happiness much more than he cared about being proven right.

It was halfway through the excellent salmon dinner that Willie mentioned the letter she had received from Amanda.

"I'm worried," she said as Matt speared a piece of broccoli.

His fork hovered above his plate as he studied her expression. She was stunning in a turquoise dress that turned her eyes dark and secretive.

"Why are you worried? She sounded happy enough to me." Amanda would tell him if she were having problems.

Willie's delicately arched brows scrunched into a frown as she poked at her salmon. "Did she tell you she hasn't found a job yet? That she hasn't made any friends?"

Matt brushed aside Willie's questions with an impatient gesture. "Yes, she said she's still looking for work and she doesn't know the neighbors yet, but that all takes time."

"I suppose you're right," Willie said slowly. "There was just something between the lines, I guess." She shrugged. "I hope I'm wrong."

"Of course you are," Matt said briskly, not wanting the pleasant mood to be broken. "Amanda is too busy to be discontented, and she's always been good at entertaining herself. I'm sure she'll make some friends before her husband leaves on that long cruise." Matt hoped she would come home for a visit then, if she hadn't found a job.

After they had finished eating, Matt took Willie's hand and led her into the lounge, where a band was playing some slow old tune that sounded vaguely familiar and blatantly romantic. Remembering how perfectly Willie fit in his arms, Matt stopped her from sitting at a small round table.

"Dance?"

Willie smiled up at him, making his breath catch somewhere in his chest. She looked wonderful, creamy shoulders bare except for a dusting of freckles and her hair shimmering like apricot silk. Wordlessly she put her hand into his as he paused to give their drink order to a passing waiter.

When they stepped onto the dance floor, Willie turned into his arms, loving the protective feel of them as he cradled her against him. She rubbed her cheek lightly against his and Matt's hand tightened on hers before he pulled her closer and clasped his hands behind her back. Willie's arms went around his neck and they moved as one to the dreamy music.

Two more numbers went by before Matt dropped his arms. When the band began to play a rousing rock song from the sixties, he shook his head.

"Let's sit this one out."

Willie couldn't help but tease him. "Too energetic for you? I thought you kept in shape."

The light of challenge gleamed in his dark eyes. "Oh, yeah? Doubting my physical abilities, are you?"

"If the shoe fits," Willie began, laughing at his expression.

Before she had time to say more, Matt had swung her around. Gazes locked, they began to dance to the driving beat.

Dancing was one of Willie's favorite activities, and she threw herself into it with enthusiasm, swinging her hips and moving her arms to the music. The way Matt's eyes widened as he watched her, his own body doing a much more subdued version of the same dance, made her warm all over. When his eyes lingered on the bodice of her dress, Willie couldn't resist a series of shimmies before she whirled away, flirting with him over her shoulder.

Matt's arm snaked around her waist, turning her back to face him. His hands stayed possessively on her hip as he smiled his appreciation at her skill.

"The justice of the peace is full of little surprises," he murmured into her ear as he leaned close. His breath on her bare skin sent a shiver to her toes and back.

"So's the stuffy lawyer," she replied, her gaze taking in the fluid movements of his powerful legs and lean hips.

Matt threw back his head and laughed. The music came to a rousing finish and he laid his arm across her shoulders, pulling her near. "Want to stay longer?" he asked, voice husky. "Or shall we stop at my house for coffee?"

Willie felt the heat rise between them as she met his dark gaze. "Do you have decaf?" she asked.

Matt pulled out his wallet and dropped several bills on the table next to their untouched drinks. "I have whatever you want," he said. "Let's go."

During the ride back to his house, Matt told her about some of his more bizarre cases. After a while conversation slowed as each became lost in his own thoughts, but Matt often reached for her hand or rested his on her knee, glancing at her and smiling. Willie trembled with anticipation each time she looked at his strong profile. *Love me*, she willed silently. *I love you.*

Matt broke the silence when he stopped in the driveway and came around to open Willie's door. He took her hand in his and bent to kiss it when she stood. "Have I told you how beautiful you are tonight?" he asked in a husky voice. "You take my breath away."

Willie reached up a hand to stroke his chest. "You told me several times, but I won't tire of hearing it. I had a lovely time."

"The night's not over," he reminded her, keeping her hand tight in his as they went through the heavy front door.

A light was burning in the entryway, and one lamp cast a circular glow in the living room beyond.

"Shall I be a good host and make the coffee?" Matt asked softly.

"Kiss me first," Willie commanded, tilting her chin. "I've missed you."

Matt needed no second invitation. He swept her into his arms and found her mouth with his. Willie trembled in his ardent embrace, parting her lips to the insistent stroking of his tongue.

After a long moment Matt stepped back, looking deep into her eyes. "You make my head spin," he said thickly. "I want everything you have to give me. I can't wait any longer."

Willie knew she had already given him more than he had requested—she had given him her heart. Reminding herself that she had to be patient, she pulled his head back down to hers.

After another sizzling kiss, Matt scooped her into his arms and carried her to the living room, setting her down on the thick rug that lay in front of the marble fireplace. Stringing kisses across her bare shoulder to the top of her dress, he reached his arms around her and began to open the zipper. Willie's fingers became busy with his tie and the buttons on his shirt. When she had freed them she ran one hand over the warm furry skin of his chest.

Matt groaned and peeled down the bodice of the turquoise dress. His breath sucked in sharply when he saw that her breasts were bare beneath it. He lowered his head, and Willie's knees went weak. Before she could recover what little sense she had left, they were entwined on the thick rug, Willie in only her panty hose and a scrap of lace panties and Matt bare chested.

He loomed over her as she caressed the width of his powerful shoulders. His hands and mouth stroked her breasts, teasing the sensitive tips into rounded buttons as she arched to give him more access. His breath against her skin was a further enticement as he slid off her remaining garments, his lips nibbling down her stomach to a sensitive hipbone.

Willie's own questing fingers lingered at his belt. When it came apart in her hands, she touched him lightly through the material of his slacks. He groaned, pushing himself against her palm. The heat of his passion made her tremble as she quickly freed him from the rest of his clothes. Then she urged him closer. When he covered her body with his, she stroked down his back to cup and massage his taut buttocks.

After a moment Matt shifted to rest on an elbow and began to stroke her lightly. Willie trembled when his gliding fingers moved across her stomach and beyond.

He leaned over to kiss her, fingers caressing her intimately until she moaned and parted her thighs.

"You feel so sweet, so welcoming," he whispered. "I want you now. Are you ready for me?"

Willie could barely answer, moving her head instead to lightly stroke his length and weigh the heavy power of his arousal. A hard shudder went through him. Then he covered her with his body as she welcomed him eagerly, and made them one.

For a moment he paused, as if savoring their closeness. Then he began to move, slowly at first. Deep within Willie an answering tremor grew, pulsating through her. Together they raced toward a powerful finale. It exploded around them as Matt held her tight, chanting her name like a prayer.

When their breathing returned to almost normal, he flopped over onto his back and pulled her against him, dropping a kiss against her hair. "Didn't even make it to the bed," he commented, running his hand down her arm.

"Two impatient people," Willie said.

"Can you stay the night?" He lifted his head to look down at her, his expression intense in the moonlight that filtered through the draperies.

Willie shook her head regretfully.

Matt didn't argue. "Then we'd better make the most of the time we have," he said as he pulled her up and over his warm body to love her again.

"YES, WARDEN, I understand." Willie listened to the voice at the other end of the line while Violet stood nearby, making a pretense of wiping off the stove.

"That will be just fine," Willie said into the receiver. "I'll see you then."

She hung up the phone and turned to her aunt, whose face bore an expression of open curiosity.

"'Warden'?" Violet echoed.

"Yes, Warden Roberts from the men's prison. We've been working together to arrange the wedding of one of the inmates." Willie allowed herself a pleased smile. "We finally have it all set and now I have the perfect third ceremony for Matt to witness."

Violet looked skeptical. "Are you sure?"

"Of course," Willie exclaimed. "It will be super. What's more romantic than a bride and groom who have been pen pals for three years and have only recently met? He proposed the first time they laid eyes on each other, and she's willing to wait for him until he gets out." She sighed. "It's a little like a fairy tale."

"Very little," Violet said dryly. "Better make sure there isn't a file in the wedding cake."

Willie refused to let her enthusiasm be dampened. "I think it's very romantic," she said. "Love at first sight. Matt will have to agree this time."

WHEN SHE MET HIM the next morning outside the opposing attorney's office, where the clients were getting together for one last attempt to settle a custody battle out of court, she was dying to tell him about the wedding. One look at his frown of concentration and she held her tongue. Soon a thin blond woman with a pale, sharp-featured face joined them in the hallway. Matt introduced Willie as his associate.

The two women shook hands briefly before the blonde, Vicky Sands, glanced over Willie's shoulder with a hiss of anger. Willie turned to see what she was looking at.

The hostility between Mrs. Sands and the man Willie guessed to be her estranged mate was almost palpable. Further introductions were made and the other lawyer, Sid Gold, chauffeured everyone inside. While his secretary served coffee, the group split into two armed camps at either end of the conference table in the large, modern office with a bay window of tinted glass.

Matt had briefed Willie about the case over the phone when they'd talked the evening before. The divorce was a bitter one. The couple had two small children, and each parent was demanding full custody. Matt was convinced the man only wanted them to spite the wife, but there was no way to prove it, and he was going to try this last time to persuade the couple to put their children's welfare above their own desire to hurt each other.

No sooner had Matt begun to talk than the husband interrupted him. "I want my kids," he said bluntly. "They don't deserve to be raised by this shrew, and we can prove it in court."

Willie thought the man's eyes were too close together, and she noticed that his fingernails were bitten to the quick.

"How?" Matt asked. "By putting your children on the stand and asking them to choose between you?"

"If necessary," his lawyer said coldly. "Kids go through it all the time. They'll get over the experience eventually."

Mrs. Sands went even paler at the attorney's words. She leaned closer to Matt and began to whisper into his ear. Her husband's face had turned a dull red and he drummed his fingers nervously.

Matt did his best to reassure his client. Her hands were clasped together, knuckles white. He was certain that deep down she and her husband both loved their children. Only their animosity toward each other had made them forget temporarily what was really important. He and Sid Gold, the other lawyer, had worked out what they hoped was a foolproof plan to remind both parents of that love. Meanwhile he would try to reason with them.

"It would be better for everyone if we could work out a satisfactory agreement here, instead of thrashing it out in court," Matt said.

The other lawyer nodded. "You never know what the judge might come up with. It could be something that neither of you wants."

His client turned and leaned close, holding up one hand like a shield as he talked earnestly in a voice too low for Matt to understand.

"What are they doing?" Vicky Sands whispered.

"I'm not sure. I wish there were some way to get through to your husband." Matt was convinced that Vicky would make a more secure home for them than her volatile husband. The hard part was convincing him to agree.

"What about shared custody?" Matt asked when Mr. Sands had straightened.

"Never!" he replied immediately.

"It's worth talking about," his lawyer said mildly.

Mr. Sands shook his head adamantly. "I won't compromise."

Matt and Sid exchanged glances.

Vicky Sands dug a tissue from her purse and dabbed at her eyes. It was all Willie could do to keep her mouth shut. She knew that Matt was doing the best he could, but impatience almost made her speak out. How could anyone put revenge ahead of his children's needs?

Matt shrugged, raking a hand through his hair. "Looks like we go for broke, then." His face was all hard lines and his jaw was thrust out with determination, but his hands were folded loosely on the table. Willie could sense his tension.

"We can beat you in court, Mr. Sands. You'll end up with nothing."

Sid spoke up. "We aren't worried. It's amazing what kids will say on the stand. Every mother has lost her temper sometime, yelled, even smacked a kid. It all comes out."

Willie hated the bland look on his face. Mrs. Sands was crying quietly.

Matt leaned forward. "And every father has said things, done things, he was ashamed of later. We can fight fire with fire."

Mrs. Sands moaned softly and her husband's frown deepened. Willie could almost feel the woman's pain. They were all treating the poor children as if they were bones to be fought over.

"We'll see who does his job better," the other attorney said. "It will all come down to what those kids say when they're questioned."

Mr. Sands frowned and turned away, muttering something to the attorney under his breath.

"Nah," Willie heard him reply. "A little counseling, perhaps, a few months in therapy, and they'll be good as new. You want custody, don't you?"

Mr. Sands hesitated, glancing at Matt, then at his estranged wife.

Matt spoke up. "I'm sure you understand what that kind of ordeal would to to your children, especially after the trauma they've already suffered from your separation." He leveled a hard stare at Mr. Sands, who stared back with a worried expression on his face.

"Either way it goes, they're bound to feel guilty." Matt glanced at Willie, his expression remote. What did he have up his sleeve?

"I know you don't want to hurt your children," he continued in a quiet voice. "Neither does Mrs. Sands. You only want to hurt each other."

The husband opened his mouth to protest, but Matt held up a silencing hand.

"You have to understand that you can't have it both ways. Either you work out an amicable compromise that puts the children's interests first, or you attack with everything you have—and harm Jeff and Molly, perhaps irreparably, in the bargain." He stopped to look at Mrs. Sands, whose head was bowed. She was crying harder, silent tears streaming down her face.

Willie longed to comfort her, but the tension in the room was so palpable she couldn't move. Why didn't Matt stop this awful conversation?

"We can win," the other lawyer urged. "I'll have those kids so confused on the stand they'll say anything."

Matt turned to the lawyer. "Sid, let's give them a few minutes alone. Either they'll kill each other, and we can put the children up for adoption—"

Mrs. Sands let out a whimper at his cold words, and Mr. Sands half rose from his chair, only to be pushed back down by his attorney.

"—or they'll decide to put the children ahead of themselves."

Sid nodded. "Good idea." He stood. "We'll give you ten minutes. Please don't get any blood on the carpet. I just had it cleaned."

Matt guided Willie out the door in front of him, herding her gently into the hallway when she would have turned back.

"You should be ashamed of yourself," she began to tell the other lawyer the minute the door was shut. "Those things you said!"

To Willie's surprise, he smiled at her. "Think it worked?" he asked. "I hope I didn't overdo it."

She glanced from him to Matt, narrowing her eyes at his smug expression. "What is this," she finally asked, "good lawyer, bad lawyer?"

Matt shrugged, subduing a grin. "I guess."

"Have you done this before?"

"Only once," Sid Gold said. "We don't oppose each other that often, but we thought it was worth a try. Might make them realize what they're doing to their kids."

"Do you think it'll work this time?" she asked nervously.

"We'll know in a minute," Matt said softly as the door to the conference room opened and Mr. Sands motioned them back inside.

"I CAN'T BELIEVE IT," Willie said to Matt, who sat across from her in the crowded seafood bar. "It worked like a charm."

Matt grinned smugly. "Yep. We had three other consultations with the parents and they were both ready to sacrifice those kids in a minute. But they didn't like hearing it from Sid. That was a very equable visiting agreement we worked out. Vicky will have the children with her—Mr. Sands can have ample visiting privileges and take them during school vacations. I don't think he'll forget about their best interests again."

"Yes," Willie agreed, "and I'm proud of your part in it."

Matt gave an exaggerated sigh. "And I suppose you have an excellent reason for this not to sway your stand on marriage one little bit."

Willie nibbled her lip. "It showed me you would never do anything that selfish," she said after due consideration. "And it made me realize something else very important."

"What's that?" Matt asked, a mildly curious expression on his face.

Willie patted his cheek. "It made me see you're going to make someone a wonderful husband."

7

WHEN WILLIE SAW the way Matt's jaw tightened and she looked into his narrowed eyes, she wished she hadn't been quite so impulsive in speaking her mind. Clearly he was not pleased to hear her latest assessment.

"Well," she said after a moment that bristled with tension, "wait until you hear where my third wedding is going to be. I can guarantee it's not someplace you've seen one held before."

She waited for him to ask where this would be, but he remained silent, staring down at the tablecloth as if he were deep in thought.

"Matt," she said impatiently, "you're not listening."

He raised his eyes to stare into hers, blinking like a person who had just awoken from a nap. "What? I'm sorry, I guess I wasn't listening."

Willie sighed. Perhaps he was preoccupied with a case, not upset over her announcement that she thought he was great husband material. When would she learn to control her tongue and think before she spoke?

"I was trying to tell you about the third wedding I've chosen for you to attend," she repeated.

Matt's sudden frown silenced her as effectively as a hand clamped across her mouth. He glanced away, drumming his fingers on the table.

"I'm not sure there's any point in my going to another one of your weddings," he said. "Sitting in on my cases didn't change your opinion of marriage, did it?"

"No, I guess not." What was he getting at?

"Well, I don't think that watching you marry people is going to change mine. I know we agreed on three each, but to tell you the truth, I think it's a big waste of time."

"Does that mean you don't want to see me anymore?" Willie asked, knotting her hands together in her lap.

Matt shook his head, and she released the breath that had caught in her throat.

"No, I'm not saying that at all. I just think there are better ways we could be spending our time." His gaze settled on her mouth, as blatant as a kiss.

Willie realized what he was getting at and her temper flared. "In bed?" she demanded.

The look Matt gave her crackled with promise. "That's one way."

Willie felt momentarily breathless. Stunned by her immediate reaction to him, she started to get up, but he grabbed her arm.

"Whoa! Don't get all offended on me now. That is something we both happen to like. Why pretend otherwise? But I didn't mean it was the only reason to keep seeing each other."

Willie leaned back in her chair and glared at him. "Oh, shucks," she said sarcastically.

Matt's devastating smile broadened and he laced his fingers through hers. "Why deny ourselves?" he asked outrageously. "We have something special going for us." Then he hesitated. "Where is this mysterious wedding going to take place, anyway?"

"I don't know if I want to tell you now."

"Come on," he coaxed. "Tell me what I'm missing."

"It's going to be at the state prison," Willie admitted reluctantly. "I just got the warden's okay, and it's set for three days from now."

Matt's expression turned incredulous. "The prison?" he echoed. "The men's maximum security prison?"

She nodded.

"You're kidding!"

Willie shook her head.

"That's dangerous."

"Nonsense."

Their gazes locked, neither willing to give in. Finally, as Willie kept glaring, Matt rubbed a hand across his forehead.

"Maybe I will go, just to make sure you get out of there in one piece."

"I'll be perfectly fine," Willie said, then clamped her lips together. If he wanted to keep a protective eye on her, who was she to argue? It was one way to get him there, and that was her main purpose.

"That's sweet of you," she murmured. "Perhaps we can ride out together."

"I'll check my calendar," Matt said warily. It was obvious he was wondering why she hadn't complained more about his proprietary attitude. Then his expression changed, as if he had come to a decision. "One way or another, I'll be there."

As it turned out, Matt was scheduled to be in court on the day of the wedding, so he told Willie he would meet her at the prison as soon as he could get away. When the judge finally adjourned his case for the day, Matt scooped the papers into his briefcase, told his client not to worry and almost ran to the parking lot.

He glanced at his watch on the way to his car, realized he was going to be late and swore under his breath as he tossed his briefcase onto the back seat. He had planned on sticking to Willie's side like a barnacle on a boat hull the whole time she was behind that high, gray wall. Now it looked as if he wasn't going to see the wedding at all; he'd be lucky to get there before she left.

Not for the first time, Matt wished she practiced real law, instead of spending her time on these weddings. On top of everything else, it would be safer. Too bad she wasn't a member of his firm, where he could at least keep an eye on her.

He was still ten minutes away from the main gate, when a news bulletin came over the car radio, chilling the blood in his veins and turning his knuckles white against the steering wheel. Swearing, he twisted the volume knob, straining for more information.

"The riot took place a short time ago at the men's prison," the announcer's voice continued cheerfully. "Hostages have been taken. We'll have more information for you as soon as it becomes available," he promised. "And now back to our Top Forty, with a selection by Whitney Houston."

Matt slammed his palm against the steering wheel, his foot pressing the accelerator closer to the floor. "I knew something would happen," he muttered, an ache beginning deep in his gut and expanding into his chest. "And I bet Willie's right in the thick of it."

He turned onto a two-lane road, taking the corner so fast the Continental fishtailed before he managed to straighten it out. Almost there. He pressed the pedal harder and the car leaped forward.

The radio announcer's voice rose again. "The latest information on that prison riot is that one civilian has been taken hostage. We don't have a name yet, but we have been told by an informed source that a woman who was at the prison to perform a wedding—"

Matt was filled with a murderous rage as he sped down the road. If anyone hurt her, he would make them sorry they'd ever drawn a breath, he vowed. If he didn't kill them with his bare hands, he would bring a case against them that would keep them behind bars for life.

When the main gate came into sight, he hit the brake hard, barely stopping before the striped barrier as a guard came out to meet him.

When the man leaned down to speak, Matt cut him off impatiently, explaining who he was and demanding to see the warden.

"JOHN," Willie said to the short, wiry convict who was pacing nervously up and down the floor of the empty supply room, "I'm sorry this happened."

He turned to stare at her, eyes watery behind wire-framed spectacles. "You women are all alike," he muttered. "Faithless, fickle broads who tromp on a man's feelings like they don't count for nothing."

"Not everyone is like Maxine."

The prospective bride had abruptly changed her mind between "dearly" and "beloved." Then, while the guards were busy breaking up a fight between two of the guests, Willie had accompanied the jilted groom to the supply room to talk.

"Just every woman I've ever met," John said morosely.

For once Willie was at a loss for words. Under the circumstances she could hardly assure him he would meet someone else who would make him forget all about the faithless Maxine. He still had ten years to serve.

Anxiously Willie watched him. How his heart must be breaking with disappointment. It would probably take him most of those ten years to regain his faith in women and in love.

"What did you want to talk to me about?" she coaxed gently. "Is there anything I can do to help?"

The rejected groom stopped his pacing and cleared his throat. "I'm sorry you came out here for nothing," he said, twisting a button on the front of the white shirt he'd worn for the wedding. "Do you think I could apply the deposit on your fee toward another ceremony?"

Willie was prevented from answering by a loud knock on the door.

MATT HAD FINALLY GAINED admittance to the huge main building of the prison complex and was rushing to the warden's office, heart in his throat. Another guard led him through a maze of hallways, then halted suddenly in front of a closed door bearing the warden's name on a brass plaque.

"Right in there," the guard said, knocking on the door.

A voice from inside called out, and the guard started to turn the knob.

Matt pushed past him, too impatient to worry about being polite. He burst into the warden's office and stopped dead, swallowing the questions that danced on his tongue.

Willie was seated in a comfortable chair across the desk from an older man Matt assumed was the warden. They both looked up at Matt expectantly as he stood gaping. Relief and anger flooded through him in equal measure, leaving him to feel like a knight who had just discovered the fire-breathing dragon had already been slain.

Willie stood. "I'm glad you made it," she said, smiling. "You missed all the excitement, but we saved you some wedding cake."

Matt reached for her, and she thrust a paper plate into his outstretched hand. He stared down at the pink-and-white frosting in confusion. Then he realized belatedly that his mouth was hanging open and closed it with a snap.

"Have a seat," Willie urged, sitting back down. "You look a little pale. The wedding's off, but we decided to cut the cake, anyway. Didn't the prison bakery do a nice job?"

Matt's knees suddenly threatened to fail him, and he sank into a chair opposite hers. The plate he was holding tipped precariously before he righted it.

Willie and the man behind the desk exchanged glances. "Matt, I don't think you've met Warden Roberts. This is a friend of mine, Matthew Bailey. He's an attorney."

"Not going to sue us, are you?" Warden Roberts asked jovially, stretching out his hand.

"That depends," Matt said, clasping it briefly. "Will one of you please tell me what happened? I heard on the radio—"

"Oh, dear," Willie said nervously. "It was just a misunderstanding. John was a little upset, but I was never in any danger."

"Oh, I don't know," the warden began, his voice tapering off when he caught the warning shake of her head. Unfortunately for her Matt saw it, too.

He set the cake down on the corner of the desk as Willie eyed him with a worried expression. He was so angry that his hands shook.

"John?" he asked.

"John Gray, the groom who was jilted." Willie's smile had become a little hesitant.

"Just what did happen?" Matt managed to ask through clenched teeth.

"The bride changed her mind—" Willie began.

"The groom lost his temper—" Warden Roberts interrupted.

"I went to the supply room with John—" Willie added.

"The convict?" Matt exclaimed, coming half out of his chair.

"Just to talk," Willie said hastily.

"The guards didn't see them leave, thought he had taken her hostage," the warden explained. "Shouldn't have jumped to conclusions, I guess."

Matt glared, and the warden's naturally ruddy complexion paled. "Unfortunately the media got hold of the story," he added.

"Anyway," Willie continued, eager, Matt had no doubt, to get off the subject of whether she had been in danger, "John wanted—"

"Sounds like you two got chummy," Matt said, his voice deadly.

"We did talk for a while. I thought he was devastated, but he only wanted to make sure my fee was transferable."

Matt's brows rose in silent query.

"For another wedding," she said. "Can you believe it?"

She and Warden Roberts were both smiling, as if the whole thing were a big joke.

"At least he recovered from the disappointment," she said cheerfully, her smile flickering, then disappearing altogether as Matt's expression remained grim.

"The bride left after giving her phone number to one of the guards," the warden said. "Nice girl, but a little scatterbrained, if you know what I mean. Flighty, not ready to settle down."

Matt hung on to his patience with everything he had.

The warden began to busy himself with rearranging the items on the top of his desk. He cleared his throat in the awkward silence.

"So we decided to eat the cake, anyway," Willie said finally, as if that summed everything up. She took another bite. "It's very good," she mumbled, mouth full. "Try it."

Matt stared at her for a long minute, willing his scattered emotions back into some semblance of order. He had been to hell and back, wondering if she was safe or dead. And now Willie was treating the whole incident as some kind of kooky adventure. He didn't know what he wanted to do more, turn her over his knee for taking such foolish chances or kiss her until he had convinced himself she was still very much alive.

The realization of just how important Willie had become in his life slammed into him with all the power of a runaway freight train, driving the breath from his lungs. He managed to retain the outward calm that served him well in the courtroom, but mentally he was reeling from shock. If Matt were inclined to believe in love, he might have mistaken this gut-twisting, brain-numbing emotion for just that. Instead he quickly reminded himself that his reaction to Willie originated in a different area of his body entirely.

Willie was beginning to look concerned as he continued to stare. Now was clearly not the time for self-analysis. Masking his feelings with effort, Matt picked up his fork and took a bite of cake.

"Not bad," he said after chewing thoughtfully.

Willie watched him closely. For a few minutes she had thought he was going to make an awful scene, but now he was accepting the warden's offer of coffee as if they were all enjoying an ordinary social visit. She sighed. His attitude might be sensible, considering that she was out of danger, but it was hardly romantic.

"Could I have some more cake?" he asked, holding his empty plate out to her.

Willie was fuming inwardly as she forced herself to smile politely and rise from the chair.

"Good coffee" she heard him say to the warden as she left the room.

He needn't have recovered quite so quickly.

MATT INSISTED on following Willie's car back to her house, where they planned to order a pizza and watch a movie on television. Willie didn't remember that Aunt Violet had gone to bingo until they walked into the empty kitchen and she saw the note lying on the table next to the mail: "Staying for both sessions. V."

Willie turned to Matt, studying his serious expression. He had barely said a word when they left the warden's office, except to agree to her suggestion of pizza and TV.

"My aunt will be gone all evening," Willie said, indicating the note. "This is double blackout night."

Matt's dark eyes began to gleam as he stared down at her. When he came closer, Willie instinctively backed up, until he felt the kitchen counter press into her back.

"We don't have to stay here," she said quickly, concerned with the deadly intent on his face. "We could go out, get burgers."

Matt shook his head slowly, eyes never leaving hers. "Oh, no," he said in a husky voice. "I have other plans."

Willie suppressed a shiver of excitement as she edged toward the doorway. Apparently his indifference had been a facade, one that was crumbling rapidly. Now his thick brows were pulled together in concentration and his brown eyes were narrowed as he stalked her.

Willie turned and glanced at the entrance to the tiny dining room, gauging her chance of escape. It hovered somewhere between slim and none. When she looked back at Matt, he was much too close, and she shifted nervously.

"What plans?" she squeaked as he stretched out one hand.

He pounced, and she shrieked as he wrapped his fingers around her upper arms and yanked her against his broad chest.

"Plans to thoroughly reassure myself that you're still in one piece," he growled, his breathing bathing her cheek as he leaned close. "I'll have to go over your delectable body inch by inch, checking for damage."

Willie's heart began to pound in double time as her wariness was replaced by a flood of response to his nearness.

"What about the pizza?" she asked, looking into his face.

With one fluid motion he picked her up and tossed her over his shoulder as if she were of no more consequence than a sack of apples. "Later," he said. "And only if you're very good."

Willie did her best.

SOMETIME LATER, after discovering that two people could fit into the narrow shower stall at the same time only if they stood very close together, Matt helped Willie back into the clothes she'd discarded so hastily.

"I hope you aren't always this sloppy," he said, picking her blouse up from the floor.

Willie colored as he studied her. She was still recovering from his lovemaking. There had been an edge of determination, of losing control, that she hadn't experienced before in his arms. Was it possible that Matt had been more concerned for her than he was willing to let on?

"If you remember, I undressed in a hurry," she said, not quite meeting his gaze. "So did you." She bent to retrieve one of his socks, which had been kicked partially beneath the bed.

He took her into his arms and nuzzled her neck, his breath tickling her sensitized skin. "Mmm, so we did. Not sorry, are you?"

Willie ducked her head. "No. Are you?"

Matt urged her chin up with one finger. "Not on your life," he whispered, meeting her mouth with his. After a moment that was too short, he broke the kiss. "I know what you really want," he teased. "Pizza."

"You're right," Willie agreed. "I seem to have worked up an appetite."

Matt didn't reply, but his smile broadened with possessive male pride as he tucked his shirttail into the waistband of his slacks.

Matt watched Willie slip her feet into sandals as he buttoned his shirt. Her cheeks were still pink and there was a softness around her eyes that he found very appealing.

"Mmm," he growled, burying his face in her hair as one hand cupped the rounded weight of her breast, "you smell like strawberries."

"Shampoo," she gasped, arching into his hand as his thumb rubbed across her sensitized nipple. Her stomach rumbled loudly, startling them both and making Matt chuckle.

"Time to satisfy another of your appetites," he teased, sliding his hand down till it rested on her stomach, as he watched a blush suffuse Willie's cheeks.

Her stomach made another rumbling noise. "Let's do something about that pizza," she said, stepping away from his loose caress.

"Of course," Matt agreed quickly. "All I had on my mind was pepperoni and black olives, honest. I'm not superman, you know."

Willie sidled up to him, sliding one hand around his waist. "Oh, I don't know about that," she murmured seductively, reaching up to kiss his cheek.

Matt caught her against his side. "How badly do you want that pizza?"

Willie's stomach rumbled again. "Badly," she echoed, eyes full of laughter.

"Keep your hands to yourself, then, while I order," Matt told her. "At the rate we're going, our dinner will be a midnight snack."

He followed her into the kitchen, where he picked up the phone to call in the order while Willie glanced through the mail.

"Here's a letter from Amanda," she said as he replaced the receiver. "Do you mind?"

Matt shook his head. "Go ahead."

She slit open the envelope and sat down to read. After a moment she put the lavender pages aside and looked up at Matt, who had been hovering curiously.

"She really sounds unhappy." Willie's voice was full of concern. She thrust the letter at Matt. "See for yourself."

"If Craig has done anything to her—" he started to bluster.

"No, I don't think it's Craig. Just read it."

Matt sat down opposite her. The phone rang and Willie got up to answer it as he began to read Amanda's neat, rounded handwriting. Before he got very far, Willie said his name, distracting him.

"What?" He frowned impatiently.

She was holding out the phone. "It's for you," she said. "It's Amanda."

He got up and took the receiver from her hand. "How are you, honey?" he asked. "How did you know to call me here?"

Amanda's voice sounded subdued. "Because you aren't here," she said. "And I know from your letters that you've been seeing a lot of Willie."

"What do you mean by 'here'?" Matt asked suspiciously. "Where are you?"

For a moment she didn't speak, and he had to curb his impatience.

"I'm home," she said in a small voice. "At your house. I've left Craig." With that startling announcement, she began to cry.

Matt's hand tightened on the receiver. He always hated it when she cried. It made him feel helpless, more so now, when he wasn't there to offer comfort.

"What is it?" Willie was asking. "Is something wrong?"

Matt covered the receiver with his hand and relayed briefly what Amanda had told him. "I'd better get home," he said with mingled regret and impatience. "Okay if I call you later?"

"Please do," Willie said, handing him his jacket. "I won't sleep a wink if you don't."

When Matt turned onto Aurora Avenue after waving at her, he couldn't even remember if he had kissed her goodbye. He was too busy thinking about Amanda and what this new development would mean.

Behind him Willie went back inside, wishing she could have gone with him. Apparently her suspicions that Amanda was having trouble adjusting to life at the base had not been just fantasy. Unless Craig had done something—something terrible.

Willie glanced at the phone, tempted to call Amanda back before Matt got there. Then she refrained. All she could do was to hope that Matt would handle the situation calmly, without flying off the handle. Amanda was extremely vulnerable. Surely Matt would realize that and treat her with consideration and understanding.

Willie was still pacing and casting baleful glances at the silent phone when Violet got home from bingo.

"Didn't expect you to be here yet," she said, locking the front door behind her. "Is Matthew with you?"

"No, he had to leave a while ago. Something came up."

Violet's brows rose. "Not having problems, are you?" she asked, slipping out of her coat and hanging it on the halltree.

Willie sighed and fluffed her hair with one hand. "We're not," she said, "but Matt's sister, Amanda, seems to be. She called him from his house earlier this evening. It seems that she's left Craig."

"My goodness," Violet exclaimed, sinking into a chair. "They've only just gotten married. People nowadays are too quick to pack. No one is interested in working things out anymore."

Willie sat across from her, nervously fingering her earring. "Matt said he'd call and let me know what happened, but he hasn't yet. I suppose they're still talking."

As if on cue, the phone rang.

Willie leaped up. "That must be him now."

Violet rose, too. "I'll leave you to talk to him while I make us some tea."

"I'm sorry to call so late," Matt said in reply to Willie's hello. "Amanda finally went to bed. She's exhausted."

"You sound tired yourself," Willie said. "Did she tell you what happened?"

Matt sighed. "I think it's the same things you tried to warn me about. I should have seen it in her letters, instead of insisting that everything was fine."

"Don't blame yourself," Willie consoled him. "She might have been consciously keeping your letters cheerier. It's not your fault. At least you're with her now when she needs you."

"It's about time, don't you think?" His voice was dry.

Willie didn't know what to say. Before she could speak, Matt continued.

"All the way home I was sure that Craig had done something unforgivable. I was ready to take him on myself, make him sorry. But Mandy and I talked a long time. I think we were able to sort out quite a bit."

Willie's heart went out to him when she heard the loving concern in his voice. "Has she decided what to do?"

She wished she could see Matt's face, be with him to soothe away the tiredness she could hear in his voice.

"She didn't say. I think she's going to sleep on it," he said.

Willie was dying to ask what advice he had given his sister, knowing his views on marriage, but there was no subtle way to frame the question. "Perhaps I could talk to her tomorrow," she offered, instead.

"Would you? I'm really at a loss. I want to help her, but I'm afraid I'll say the wrong thing and she'll clam up for good."

So am I, Willie thought, remembering how insistent he had been that Amanda not marry Craig to begin with. It would be easy for him to encourage their split now, thinking it was right for her. But the last thing Amanda needed to hear was an "I told you so."

"Should I come over there?" she asked, wondering if Matt was going to stay home with Amanda. Willie really wanted to talk to the younger girl alone.

"Mandy planned to visit you in the morning. I have to be in court, but she has her own car. She said something last night about going back, but I don't know if it's for good. She's awfully confused."

Willie could hear the tension in Matt's voice. She knew he loved his sister, but she was also well aware of the way he felt about Amanda's marriage. She was vulnerable now, and Matt could easily persuade her to do something unwise.

"I'll wait until I hear from her, then," Willie said, stifling her impatience. "My whole morning is open. I was going grocery shopping, but that can wait until later."

"Okay. Get some sleep now. That's what I'm planning to do. It's been a long day for both of us."

Willie remembered the incident at the prison and had to agree. There had been a few minutes when she hadn't known what John would do, and now she realized she really was exhausted.

"Good night," she said.

"Willie?" His voice had softened.

"What?"

"I'm glad everything worked out okay today."

The caring in his tone made her smile. "Thanks. Me, too." Willie hung up the receiver and glanced at the grandfather clock. It was time to go to bed if she hoped to have her wits about her the next day.

IT WAS MIDMORNING when Amanda arrived. When the bell rang, Willie flung open the door and gave her a big hug.

"It's so good to see you," Willie said as they both went inside. "I made coffee. Come sit in the living room and have a piece of Aunt Violet's blackberry bread. We picked the berries last fall and froze them." She realized she was rattling, not allowing Amanda to get a word in, so she clamped her lips together while they both sat down.

"It's nice to see you again," Amanda said in her soft voice. Willie poured coffee and handed her a cup.

There was a short silence while they both sipped the hot brew. Willie noticed there were dark smudges beneath Amanda's eyes, and she seemed very tense.

"How have you been?" she asked. "I've enjoyed your letters."

Amanda's gaze flicked to Willie, then down to the faded roses on the carpet. "Matt must have told you why I came home," she said, stirring her coffee. "I feel so silly about it now."

"Yes," Willie admitted. "He did tell me after you called here. Would it help to talk about it?"

"Matt and I talked for a long time last night."

Willie felt a sinking sensation.

"He made me see that I have to give it another chance," Amanda said, surprising her. Willie had expected Matt to encourage Amanda to make the split permanent.

"He did?" She couldn't hide the shock in her voice.

Amanda smiled. "It's not what you expected to hear, is it? Me, neither. Knowing how dead set against the marriage Matthew was, I expected him to back me up. Instead he pointed out a few things I hadn't considered."

"Like what?" Willie asked.

Amanda stared at her hands, which she was twisting nervously. "Craig's gone a lot," she said. "I got so lonesome. I couldn't find a job, and I didn't know anyone." She shrugged.

"Haven't you met any of your neighbors?" Willie asked.

"They came over when we first moved in, but all I wanted was Craig. Then when he was gone I felt funny calling after I had ignored their overtures. Matt made me understand that I have to make friends. Craig's going to be gone for six months soon when the ship goes to Australia. There will be other wives on the base whose husbands are gone, too. We'll have to stick together." She tucked a strand of light brown hair behind her ear.

"That's true," Willie said.

Amanda bobbed her head in agreement. "Matt reminded me that I made a commitment and that I haven't tried very hard to adjust. Instead I've put the responsibility for my happiness on Craig, and that's not fair." She took a deep breath.

Willie's heart soared at Amanda's words. Could it be Matt was changing? She could only hope so.

"So I'm going back," Amanda said. "I'm going to keep looking for a job, and in the meantime, I'm going to volunteer at the base day-care center. It will give me some experience with kids—" she colored slightly "—for when we have our own family. And I'm going to make some friends."

"You sound very determined," Willie said. "Is there anything I can do to help?"

Amanda smiled. "Craig's out on sea trials, so he won't have to know how foolish I've been." She took another sip of coffee. "Keep writing," she said. "I want us to stay friends."

"Of course. Me, too."

"I feel as if a big weight has been taken off my shoulders," Amanda said. "I'm glad I came home and talked to you and Matt."

"Me, too. And I think you've made the right decision." Willie began to relax. The crisis was over.

Amanda took another slice of blackberry bread. "Now what's this I hear about you dating my brother?" she asked.

8

AMANDA'S QUESTION had caught Willie off guard, and she took a sip of her coffee while she tried to think of the best way to answer.

"Do you mind that we're seeing each other?" she finally asked.

"Heck, no!" Amanda exclaimed. "I think it's terrific. In fact, I wish I'd thought of introducing you myself. It would be great if my two favorite people got together, you know what I mean?"

Willie knew all too well. The thought of getting together with Matt had occurred to her more than once, too.

"Don't get carried away," she cautioned. "Matt and I are just friends, and our ideas are really very different."

A tiny frown marred Amanda's smooth forehead. "Ideas about what?" she asked.

"About marriage, for one thing." Willie felt her cheeks go hot. "You know how he feels about that."

Amanda rolled her eyes. "That was before," she said. "Maybe you're the reason he encouraged me to give my marriage another chance." She clapped her hands together with enthusiasm. "Maybe he loves you. Has he told you? Are you serious about each other?"

Willie hesitated, unsure how to answer. The words that they were "just friends" had almost stuck in her throat. Sometimes she wanted to shout her love to the skies, and at other times she understood that she had to be patient, until Matt realized he loved her, too. Still, it was hard not to tell Amanda the truth about her feelings.

Amanda's expression changed suddenly, her excitement turning to dismay. "I'm sorry," she said. "I didn't mean to be so personal. I just got so excited at the idea of you two together. You're perfect for Matt."

Willie couldn't stop herself from asking why.

"He needs someone like you," Amanda said. "He's so serious, so stuffy sometimes. Maybe seeing so many unhappy clients has, I don't know, twisted him in some way. Our parents' marriage left more scars on him because he was older. I don't remember their fights as much as he does." She leaned closer confidingly. "You'd make him lighten up."

Willie was tempted to ask what Matt was supposed to do for her while she was brightening up his life, but restrained herself.

"Well," she said, deliberately changing the subject, "are you going back to the base right away?"

Amanda smiled, twisting her wedding ring around her finger. "Yes," she said. "I have a lot to do before Craig gets back. I don't want him to ever find out how foolish I've been." Her expression said that for now, at least, the crisis was past.

"Keep in touch," Willie told her as Amanda rose and preceded her to the door. "You know how much I care about you."

They hugged and Amanda thanked her for the coffee and blackberry bread. Before she left, she promised to bring Craig by to see Willie and her aunt as soon as he got back.

While Willie was picking up their dishes, she couldn't help but wonder about the advice Matt had given his sister. Perhaps her weddings had influenced him, even if he hadn't gotten around to admitting it yet. The thought cheered her, making even the prospect of grocery shopping, which she normally detested, a pleasant task.

WHEN THE DOOR to his office opened and Amanda breezed in, Matt looked up from the work spread before him on the desk.

"I wanted to say goodbye," she said, bending to give him a hug. "Thanks for putting me up and for putting up with me, too."

He sat back in his chair, studying her face, which had lost the tenseness and pallor of the night before. "You look happier than the last time I saw you. But why are you saying goodbye?"

Amanda beamed. "I'm going home."

Matt's brows rose and she chuckled. "Home to Craig," she clarified.

Matt steepled his fingers under his chin. "You decided that awfully quickly."

She shrugged, sitting on the corner of his desk. "After we talked and I did some thinking, it all fell into place," she said. "Perhaps you're in the wrong business. Ever thought of being a marriage counselor?"

Matt returned her grin, shaking his head. "I can truthfully say I've never thought of that. But I'm glad to see you smiling again."

"Thanks to you."

He spread his hands. "What can I say? You came to the right place. But are you sure you have to leave right away? We could go somewhere really nice for dinner this evening."

Amanda shook her head. "Thanks, but there are a lot of things I want to do back home. Besides, you could always take Willie to dinner, instead."

He ignored her comment. "Did you two have a nice visit?"

"Oh, yes. She's very special, isn't she?" Amanda probed.

Matt suppressed a smile at her lack of subtlety. "She's quite a woman," he agreed solemnly, giving away nothing.

"I'm glad you appreciate her," Amanda said. "You know, now that I've settled down, you should think about it yourself."

"Whoa," Matt said, straightening. "Let's get one thing clear."

"What?" Amanda's smile was patently innocent.

"No matchmaking!"

"Okay," Amanda agreed after a moment.

"Promise?" He didn't like the way her eyes were twinkling.

"I promise."

After Amanda left, he swiveled his chair around so that he was looking out the window. His office had a beautiful view of the waterfront and the Olympic Mountains far away in the mist of the peninsula, but he scarcely noticed as he chewed absently on his pen and thought about Willie.

Somewhere along the line she had slipped beneath his defenses without his realizing it. What had seemed like a simple plan to have a brief, mutually beneficial affair had somehow become much more complicated. Still, he told himself that all the things he had said to Amanda about love being worth some effort and compromise didn't apply to him .

He hoped Amanda would be one of the lucky ones and have a happy marriage, but he knew from painful experience that love and all that went with it wasn't for him. He had tried once, only to find out he was just like his parents. Failure hurt, and he wasn't dumb enough to let himself be hurt again. When it came to commitment, he told himself he would never be ready, even for a woman as lovable as Willie.

TWO WEEKS PASSED. Willie saw Matt several times, going back to his house to make sweet, heated love with him. Each time she became more deeply involved, more hopeful that he, too, was beginning to see that they were made for each other.

If the fiery way they came together was any indication, they were perfectly suited. Matt was by turns tender, masterful and overwhelmingly passionate. Each time with him revealed another facet of his lovemaking. Willie felt more feminine, more desirable, than she had ever dreamed possible. When she was alone, just thinking about Matt's kisses and his caresses was enough to make her wish he were with her so she could show him how much she loved him.

She was alone one afternoon, making cookies for the senior center, when the phone rang. Even before she picked it up, some sixth sense told Willie it was Matt.

"I wish this association meeting weren't tonight," he grumbled after they said hello. "There are things I'd rather be doing."

"I can't imagine what," Willie teased. "I'm looking forward to an evening of reruns myself."

"I think I'm offended." Matt's voice grew husky. "I wish I were with you right now." His voice grew even deeper as he began to describe what he'd like to do to her.

"First I'd find all the places you dab that scent that drives me wild," he murmured, "and I would kiss every one."

Willie felt the heat building in her, fueled by his words and the need in his voice. Her eyes drifted shut.

"I'd run my hands over that soft skin of yours, and I'd pay special attention to all the places that made you shiver when I touched them before."

Willie swallowed hard, ear glued to the receiver.

"I'd undress you slowly, then you'd undress me."

The image of his powerful body brought a moan up from her throat. She stifled it with knuckles gone white.

"Then I'd lower you to the bed—" Matt's voice trembled to a stop on an uneven rasp of breath.

Willie felt as if she were on fire. She could even smell the smoke. It took a moment for her to remember where she was.

"Oh!" she exclaimed, "The cookies are burning!" She dropped the phone and yanked open the oven door.

"Sorry," she said when she had picked up the receiver again. "They're only burned on the bottom. I think I can save them."

"I guess I distracted you," Matt said, sounding smug. "I better get to why I called before you burn anything else."

"Good idea."

"Tomorrow night," he said. "Very special evening. Wear something classy. Not that you don't always look spectacular, but this is a very important occasion."

"Is that all you're going to tell me?" Willie cried after a moment of silence. "Where are we going? What's up? Why is it so special? It's not my birthday."

"That's all I'm saying. Trust me."

Her diligent coaxing couldn't get another word out of him, and she finally gave up. Reluctantly she said goodbye. Curiosity was eating her alive as absently she bit into a cookie while puzzling over what he'd said.

Could it be that Matt was going to admit his feelings were as strong as her own? Ask her to share his future? She plunked down distractedly on a kitchen chair. Try as she might, she couldn't think of anything else it could be.

Tomorrow evening was going to take forever to arrive!

THE NEXT AFTERNOON she raced home from a wedding at the beach to get ready for their special date. If Matt was going to tell her what she thought he was, she wanted to look her best for him, from the skin out. She took a quick shower and shampooed the sand from her hair before slipping into satiny undies trimmed with a wide border of delicate lace. Thinking about how the two of them would intimately celebrate their mutual happiness made her flush with excitement as she blow-dried her hair. What they shared was very special and she could hardly wait to see him again.

"You look fantastic," Matt told her when she opened the door to him early that evening. His warm gaze lingered on the deep vee neckline of her dark-green-and-white polka-dot dress before it skimmed down the full skirt to her slim legs and high-heeled black patent shoes. Then he returned his attention to her face.

With the dark green dress Willie wore gold heart-shaped earrings and a matching locket on a thin chain, which had once been her mother's. Her only real concession to the outrageous streak in her nature was the gold serpentine bracelet with its two gleaming emerald eyes, which circled her right wrist.

Willie gave Matt a quick hug, her hands stroking the shoulders of his black suit and her nostrils flaring to absorb the sharp lime scent of his cologne. "I missed you," she murmured, stepping back. "I've been looking forward to this evening."

"So have I." His eyes danced with excitement as he pulled her into his arms with obvious intent.

Willie tipped her head up for his kiss, but she wasn't prepared for the response that rose within her like a tidal wave at the first touch of his mouth on hers. When her lips parted, Matt groaned and deepened the kiss with a thrust of his tongue. It was a long, breathless moment before Willie remembered where they were, and another moment before she reluctantly broke the embrace.

Matt's eyes had darkened, and he looked as if he were going to take her in his arms again. Instead he ran a hand through his hair and took a deep breath.

"Tonight is going to be really special," he promised.

"But you didn't tell me where we're going. I hope I'm dressed okay."

"Perfect. And you'll find out soon enough what I have planned," he teased, tapping her nose with his finger. "You know what happened to the curious cat."

She couldn't resist fluttering her lashes at him provocatively. "I remember what brought it back," she murmured, snuggling close.

"Good evening, Matthew," Aunt Violet said as she came down the hallway from her bedroom. "Don't you look dashing."

When Willie disentangled herself from the arm he had curled around her shoulders, he made a courtly bow, smiling broadly. "Thank you, ma'am. And may I say that you are an absolute vision."

Willie was delighted to see that his compliment had momentarily flustered her normally unflappable aunt, who smoothed down the pleated skirt of the blue-and-white paisley dress she was wearing with a large corsage of artificial pink flowers pinned to the front. For a change her white hair was untinted, and shone in the overhead light like spun sugar.

"This old thing," she said deprecatingly, straightening the dress's lace collar. Then she asked, "Where are you off to this evening?"

Willie turned to Matt expectantly.

"Ah," he said. "It's a surprise. Willie will have to fill you in later."

"Have a nice time, then," Violet said. "I'm going to watch a couple of old movies on the television with a gentleman friend."

"As long as he's a gentleman, I won't worry about you," Matt told her as Willie grabbed her purse and a lacy shawl. "Don't wait up for this beauty tonight. I plan to keep her out very late."

It was Willie's turn to be flustered as Matt escorted her to his car.

"Where are we going?" she repeated as he headed the Lincoln toward the downtown area.

Matt named an elegant restaurant at the top of one of the tall office buildings that had sprung up recently, altering the skyline of downtown Seattle. "I hope you like it," he added, glancing at her as he turned onto the freeway entrance.

Willie rested her hand on his thigh, feeling how the powerful muscles contracted beneath her touch. "It sounds wonderful," she said. "But, then, I like anywhere that you take me."

There was no question he had something in mind, and Willie was sure she knew what it was. He fairly thrummed with excitement. What a romantic place to propose, high above the lights of the city. Would he ask her there, she wondered, or wait until later on when they were alone together at his house? Anticipation made it difficult to sit still as the car sped down the road.

When they walked through the wide doorway of the elegant dining room, the maître d' came forward to greet them.

"Bailey," Matt told him. "Party of six."

Willie's steps faltered. Six?

With a reassuring smile, Matt touched his hand to her elbow as Willie followed the maître d' to their table. To her utter confusion, she saw two couples already seated there, strangers to her. Did Matt need witnesses? The two men rose, smiling, as she and Matt approached.

Willie hesitated, but he urged her forward, his hand sliding to the small of her back. As she glanced at him, puzzled, he made quick introductions.

"Willie, I'd like you to meet Jim and Nellie Parker, Rod and Ann Westover. You may remember them from Amanda's reception. Willie Webster, the lawyer I told you about."

Willie acknowledged the others, her head buzzing with confusion. What an odd way to introduce her.

"Jim and Ann are both partners in my firm," Matt explained after he had pulled out Willie's chair and they were all seated. "I wanted you to meet again socially so you could get to know one another better."

"Why?" Willie asked baldly. Her hope that Matt had chosen this evening, this restaurant, to pop the question was fading as fast as a vacation suntan. She twisted her fingers together in her lap, waiting for him to reply.

Instead of enlightening her, Matt ordered drinks all around, then proceeded to make small talk until they each had a glass in hand. Then, without warning, he delivered the killing blow to her expectations.

"You know that I've felt all along you could be making better use of your law degree," he said as the others looked on, smiling politely. "I've been thinking of a way to fix that, and I think I've come up with a mutually beneficial idea." He beamed at Willie.

"I wanted my associates to meet you," he continued. "Perhaps the idea of working together has already occurred to you, but I wanted to make an official offer."

Willie was stunned by his words.

"We've talked over your qualifications, and I'm proud to be extending to you the opportunity to come in with us. I would like you to join the firm."

Willie felt her face go stiff as he raised his glass and took a sip. Four glasses followed his example. Four attractive faces stared at Willie, waiting, no doubt, for her to speak.

"Join the firm?" she croaked.

"Yes," Matt said, smiling broadly at her confusion. "A chance to practice real law, with the opportunity for a full partnership in the future." He was clearly pleased with himself and his announcement as he glanced around the table.

Willie took a large drink of her strawberry margarita, stalling for time. Her brain seemed to have shut down and her tongue forgotten how to function. She managed to swallow past the sudden lump in her throat before she focused dazed eyes back on Matt.

"Well?" he prompted eagerly. "What do you think?"

Willie resisted the urge to open her mouth and howl with disappointment, but barely.

"I'm speechless," she finally said in a flat voice. "I think I need some time to digest your offer."

If Matt was disappointed with her lack of enthusiasm, he didn't show it.

The part about being speechless was true. Her plea for time was an outright fabrication. She needed no time at all to decide what to do about his offer. Only the deeply ingrained manners of a minister's daughter kept her from telling him in front of his business associates what he could do with it. That and the self-preservation that refused to let her release the control she was clinging to and make a scene. Without those constraints, she would have gladly given in to the sudden, burning urge to flip Matt over her shoulder through one of the windows that looked down onto the street, forty-six floors below.

Instead she managed to select an item from the elegant menu the waiter set in front of her, make small talk with the other two couples and mask the fury coursing through her.

Willie thought the meal would never end as she listened to the lawyers discuss cases. Jim's wife had two small children, whose pictures she was more than willing to show Willie. Ann's husband was a stockbroker. Except for asking one or two polite questions, Willie was content to let the others talk while she pushed the food around her plate. More than once she felt Matt's gaze on her, but she steadfastly refused to meet it. He probably thought she was overwhelmed. Finally, after coffee for everyone, the interminable meal ended.

"It's been lovely meeting you," Ann Webster said. "I hope we'll be seeing you at the office soon."

"I'll have to talk to Matt some more before I decide," Willie said lamely. "I do have a fairly busy practice now."

Ann nodded, obviously surprised that Willie would give her "offbeat weddings" another thought in the face of such a dazzling opportunity. "Of course," she murmured politely.

If they had expected Willie to leap on Matt's suggestion like a cat on a fat sardine, they would just have to be disappointed.

"Nice meeting you," Jim Parker said, rising to leave. "If you have any questions that old Matt can't answer, give me a call. Here's my card."

Willie glanced at Nellie, but she was smiling encouragingly. "You could do worse," she said, picking up her purse.

After goodbyes all around, Matt turned to Willie, an odd expression on his face. It was plain that her reaction, or rather lack of one, had disappointed him. "More coffee, or a drink?" he asked, studying her closely.

"No, thank you," Willie said, allowing a tiny bit of her anger to seep out. "I think we need to talk. Privately."

Matt dealt with the check. "I see." Clearly he did not see, or he would never have considered doing what he had.

It was obvious to Willie now that he didn't understand or even know her at all. The realization of how little the ceremonies she had shared with him meant cut more deeply than anything else. Without looking to see if he was following, she stalked from the restaurant across the foyer to the bank of elevators and stabbed the down button.

They walked to the car and Matt drove in silence back to the north end of Seattle, sneaking wary glances in Willie's direction.

"Where shall we go?" he asked finally, completely puzzled by her odd behavior.

He had imagined that by this time in the evening they would have been busily discussing her move. He had pictured himself telling her about the firm as she made plans to close down her little wedding business and join him. He had even toyed with the idea of asking her to move in with him, before sanity returned and he realized that one major change at a time was enough for both of them.

Combining business with pleasure could prove sticky and he wanted to make sure Willie's transition back to real law would be smooth and without distractions. They could go on as they were until she had settled in at the office. He had already resigned himself to the realization that the fire that burned between them wasn't going to be doused quickly, but he was still leery of even a living-together arrangement. It smacked of commitment. Willie had become the most important thing in his life, even pushing his love for Mandy to the sidelines, and he wanted nothing to spoil that.

"Aunt Violet is entertaining," Willie reminded him. "We might as well go to your house." Somehow her wording was not conducive to Matt's earlier expectations or a mutually satisfying end to the evening.

Now, as he turned into his driveway, he sent another worried glance in Willie's direction. Her profile was all he saw. She was staring ahead as if the landscaping fascinated her. He could feel her tension and, for the first time, began to have doubts about what he'd done.

Perhaps Willie thought he should have made the offer in private, instead of springing it on her in front of the others. He had only wanted her to meet some of the people she would be working with, and wanted them to meet her. As senior partner he had the final vote in hiring, and the others always went along with him, but he thought it was a nice gesture to introduce everyone socially. Glancing again at her aloof expression before he climbed from the car, he wasn't so sure.

When he reached out a hand to her, he gripped icy fingers. As soon as she could, she pulled away from his loose hold, fussing with the shawl she had slipped across her shoulders earlier. Her eyes hadn't willingly met his since they had left the restaurant. Still, perhaps she was just deep in thought. Changing jobs was a big step.

Once Matt had turned on the lights and they were standing in the center of his living room, he reached for Willie's shawl.

"Don't touch me," she grated. She backed away, eyes blazing, and Matt realized she wasn't overwhelmed at all. She was downright red-faced, teeth-grinding furious.

"Would you like to sit down?" he asked cautiously.

"No!" Her hands were curled into fists and her hair seemed to crackle with a life of its own as she stalked over to where he stood and tipped back her head to glare into his face. At that point Matt knew he had made a serious error in judgment.

"Tell me again how I'm wasting my degree," Willie said in a chilling voice he barely recognized. "I don't think I quite absorbed the full significance of your statement earlier. I was too stunned by your *generous* offer." She bit off each word as if it were something offensive, her even, white teeth almost snapping together.

"I, uh—" Matt began, his usual smooth rhetoric deserting him.

"Then tell me again what a favor you're doing, offering me a job with your divorce mill!"

Her eyes were shooting sparks, the green in them all but gone in the haze of cold, steely gray.

"'Divorce mill'?" Matt echoed, offended. "Just a—"

"*Then*," Willie gritted, her voice rising, "tell me what a wonderful opportunity you've presented me to go around destroying marriages the way you do!" Now she was shouting.

"I wouldn't put it quite like that," Matt argued. To his surprise, she didn't cut him off this time. "You'd be doing a lot of good, and you would have interesting, challenging cases to stimulate your brain." He was tempted to add that she would be doing more than reciting vows by rote over and over, but one look at her expression and he decided not to go for overkill.

"Well," Willie said after a short pause. "I want to thank you very much for your offer. Not that I would consider accepting it for a millisecond, mind you. But because I'm glad I found out how you still think of me and what I do."

Her chin came up and she gave him a look that reminded him of the way opposing counsel sometimes tried to intimidate him before a case. As if he were so far off the mark he didn't have a prayer. Usually he ignored tactics like that. Tonight he found he couldn't.

"Wait a minute," he said as Willie turned and began to walk away. "Where are you going?"

"I'm going to call a cab," she said, surprising him. "If I can use your phone."

"Of course," he answered automatically. "Wait a minute!" he exclaimed as she picked up the receiver. "There's no reason for you to do that. Aren't you going to stay with me?"

Her expression could have flash-frozen a side of beef. "Not for all the money in Fort Knox," she said.

Matt winced. "Can't we talk about this?"

"You really expect me to spend the night with someone who understands me as poorly as you do?" she asked. "No way, buddy."

"Just a minute," Matt said. "I thought we had something special between us. I thought you liked spending time with me."

"So did I. That was when I thought you understood me, that you cared about me and what I am."

Matt frowned, confused. "You like me," he argued. "You want me. I know what you felt in my arms."

Willie flushed, her freckles disappearing in the wash of color. "I was foolish enough to think you had a romantic streak," she said. "I guess I saw what I wanted to, trying to mold you into the hero I needed you to be."

Matt took a step toward her, but she backed up with unflattering haste. He stopped. "I can be romantic," he said. "Just tell me what you want."

Willie thought for a moment. "My ideal hero is the total opposite from you," she said finally. "I want a man to sweep me off my feet. I want a swashbuckling pirate with a cutlass in his teeth and a gold ring in his ear who will carry me off in his arms. And to hell with the consequences." Her expression turned scornful. "I want a man so different from you that *you* couldn't even imagine him."

Matt remained silent until she turned away and opened the phone book to the Yellow Pages. When she began to dial, he snapped out of the stunned trance her angry words had created and moved quickly, depressing the button on the phone.

"This is silly," he said, accepting that further conversation that evening was probably pointless. "I'll take you home."

Without comment she headed for the front door, turning, after she'd opened it, to see if he was coming. Matt whipped his keys out of his pants pocket and followed her. When she cooled off she would realize what she'd be missing if she turned down his offer, he tried to reassure himself. Perhaps he hadn't gone about things in the best way, but his intentions were sound. All her crazy talk about pirates and romantic heroes was just temper. She would come around. He nibbled on his lower lip. Of course she would.

Willie got into the passenger side of the car before he could reach out to open her door for her. Annoyed himself now, he got behind the wheel and took her home, the music on FM radio the only sound in the car's luxurious interior.

Willie leaped out before they had completely stopped, forcing herself to turn and recite a polite little "Thank you for dinner" before she slammed the car door behind her. Matt's expression revealed nothing as he stared up at her. Willie half hoped he would follow and try to apologize, but before she was even up the steps, the squeal of tires told her he had driven off.

Willie shrugged, trying to tell herself it was just as well. She blinked away the sudden tears that threatened to spill from her eyes, sniffed, and went inside.

"You catching a cold?" Aunt Violet asked when Willie said hello to her and her friend.

"Maybe. I'll take some vitamin C when I go to bed." She answered a couple of questions about the evening while managing not to reveal what a disaster it had been, and retreated to her room. It was hardly the way she had expected the evening to end.

It was very late, but Willie wasn't sleeping when she heard the front door close on Aunt Violet's gentleman friend. A few minutes later there was a soft knock on her bedroom door.

"Come in," she said, wondering what her aunt wanted.

Violet opened the door and stuck her white head inside. "I didn't wake you, did I?"

"No," Willie said, sitting up and turning on her bedside lamp. "Did you want to talk?"

Violet stepped farther inside, the look on her face one of concern. It dashed Willie's hopes that her aunt merely wanted to discuss her own evening. Willie didn't think she was up to talking about Matt and what had happened. The pain was still too raw.

"You didn't appear to have gotten what you wanted tonight when you came in to say hello," Violet said, sitting on the corner of Willie's bed. "I wondered if you'd like some cocoa."

They had shared many a late-night cup of cocoa while Willie was growing up. Aunt Violet had filled in for the mother who had died before her time on more than one occasion, and Willie couldn't hurt her by refusing now.

"That would be nice."

"It will only take me a moment," Violet said, getting up. "You stay put and I'll bring it."

While she was gone, Willie took a drink of water, smoothed her hair and slipped into a worn chenille bathrobe. She had a wedding in the morning, but knew she wouldn't have gone to sleep right away, anyway.

When Violet returned with a tray, they seated themselves in old-fashioned chairs on either side of a small table Willie had brought from her father's parsonage. Her mother had kept it sitting in the front hallway, with fresh flowers or an arrangement of dried weeds in a vase on its inlaid wood surface. Having the little table in her room made Willie feel close to both parents.

Violet had put marshmallows in the cups just as she had when Willie was younger. For a moment they each stirred their cocoa silently. Willie knew Violet was waiting in her patient way for her to begin.

Taking a swallow of cocoa, Willie proceeded to tell Violet about her expectations for the evening and what had actually occurred.

"I feel so foolish," she confessed. "I had such hopes." Tears threatened to choke her and she hastily sipped at her cocoa again before continuing to recite what had taken place. It was her own fault that she was disappointed, but she couldn't forgive Matt for reading her so wrong.

"I can see why you're upset with him," Violet said when Willie had finished talking. "Of course, you had a fair idea of the man when you started seeing him." She took a sip from the bone china cup.

"I know." Willie sighed. "But I thought he was changing." She made a helpless gesture. "I wonder how many women have said those same words over the past twenty centuries. Why do we always seek to change the men we love?"

"Because we want what's best for them?" Violet guessed with a gentle smile. "I don't know, dear. Are you sure that things are really over with Matthew?"

Willie nodded emphatically. "He doesn't understand me at all. And I can't say that I understand him, either. I know about his background, his parents and his own divorce. But he's an intelligent man. He could reason things out and realize he's being too inflexible."

Violet reached over to pat Willie's tightly clenched fist. "You mean, if he were smart enough, he could change himself so you wouldn't have to do it?" she asked.

"Is that what I'm doing?" Willie picked up her half-full cup, turning it around and around. "Not that it matters anymore. Matt and I are definitely through."

"But you love him," Violet guessed, reaching for Willie's hand.

Before Willie could pull away, Violet was studying her palm. "I don't think we've seen the last of Mr. Bailey," she mused. "But it's hard to get a clear picture here. Perhaps we'll just have to wait and see what happens."

When Willie had washed out their cups and climbed back into bed, determined to get a little sleep before morning, she went back over Aunt Violet's last words. It was difficult not to get her hopes up, but Willie prided herself on knowing when to be realistic. She couldn't see either Matt or her changing enough to make a difference. She had been right earlier; he was as far away from a romantic hero as any man could be and still remain a human male. *Except for the way he kissed and made love,* a naughty little voice inside her whispered.

"Don't remind me," Willie groaned out loud.

With a sigh, she pulled the blanket over her head. Forgetting Matt when she loved him the way she did was going to be hard. Maybe Violet had a potion among her herbs that would help.

9

WILLIE WAS NOT SURPRISED when Matt didn't call, but she was bitterly disappointed. A single candle flame of hope inside her didn't want him to give up so easily.

"You getting enough sleep?" Aunt Violet asked Willie one morning as she slipped a navy robe and matching high-heeled shoes into her garment bag in preparation for a formal wedding at a prestigious and private local tennis club.

"Of course," Willie said. "Haven't I always slept like a baby?"

Violet peered at the circles beneath Willie's eyes that Willie herself had been studying earlier. "Humph," the older woman said. "Why don't you just call him and straighten this mess out."

Willie refrained from the obvious question, "Call who?" They both knew what Violet was talking about. If Matt was waiting for Willie to call, he could wait forever. She had created for herself a full, satisfying life before he'd come along, and she could have that again. All it took was a little concentration, some willpower and a talent for blocking out the pain she was beginning to think would stay with her forever.

"I'll be back before one," Willie told her aunt. "I have two weddings here this afternoon, and the florist promised to deliver fresh flowers sometime this morning." Willie always liked to have bouquets in the parlor, where she performed the weddings. A lot of people took pictures and the flowers added a nice touch.

"I'll be here," Violet said in a resigned voice. "I suppose the parlor could stand a vacuuming while I'm waiting for the florist."

Willie knew her aunt was slightly disgruntled at her niece's refusal to do anything about Matt, but she couldn't help that. Violet would have to get used to his absence in their lives, just as she was trying to do. In a way it was painful to see so much joy reflected on the faces of the people she joined together. She wondered if Matt ever thought about her when he was dissolving marriages, but she doubted it would be as difficult as seeing these happy couples and knowing that she herself might never have that kind of special relationship.

"You're a dear," she said, giving her aunt a hug.

Another "Humph" followed her out the door.

When Willie got home from what she privately thought of as the wedding of the year, the parking area in front of the chapel was so full she had to park around the side. She hoped her parlor would hold what was obviously a large wedding party. She hadn't meant to cut things so close, but when the last bride's sister had wanted to discuss hiring Willie for her own posh wedding in six months it had seemed prudent to hang around.

Getting out of her Corvair, Willie glanced at her watch. At least she wasn't actually late. Not quite.

Aunt Violet emerged from the parlor, where she had been serving tea, when Willie came through the front door.

"I have a surprise for you," she said, carrying the silver tray toward the kitchen.

Willie glanced at the crowded parlor. "I see that."

"No, no," Violet said. "The surprise is in the living room."

Willie went in curiously, and before she could even say hello, Amanda jumped up and hugged her. Craig was right behind her, looking tanned and fit.

"What a great surprise," Willie said, returning Amanda's embrace and giving Craig a quick kiss. "How long can you stay?"

"We're having dinner with Matt," Amanda said. "Do you want to come with us?"

There was an uncomfortable silence.

"Have you talked to him yet?" Willie asked.

"Just to tell him we were coming over," Craig said. "Is there a problem?"

"No, no." Willie didn't want to upset them when they were obviously so happy. "I'm just tied up tonight, that's all."

Amanda looked disappointed. "We should have called ahead," she said. "But we have three days. Are you busy tomorrow?"

"Just in the morning. How about lunch?"

Craig and Amanda exchanged a quick glance. "Great," she said.

"I have a wedding to do now," Willie explained as the grandfather clock began to chime. "Can you wait here until I'm done and then we can talk some more?"

MATT HAD BEEN GLAD when Mandy had called to tell him she and Craig were coming for a visit. Perhaps they could take his mind off Willie and the fact that he missed her so much. What a hell of a time to discover that what he felt for her was probably love. He couldn't think of anything else that could make him so lonely, miserable and could completely erase his power to concentrate. He hadn't realized until it was too late how much his views on love had changed since he'd first met her. He had let his work warp his attitude, not taking into account that he saw only the failed relationships in his office. It had been easy to forget about all the relationships that did not fail, the couples he would never see professionally.

He'd had a couple of awkward moments when he'd called a witness "Willie" in court and once when he'd been thinking about her so hard he'd almost missed the judge's instruction for him to give his closing arguments.

Maybe spending the evening with his sister and her husband would block out thoughts of a certain freckled redhead and the passion she could draw from him so effortlessly. Matt glanced down at the scratch pad he'd been doodling on to see that he had been writing "Matt and Willie" over and over.

It was much later that evening, after Mandy and Craig had gone up to the guest room, that Matt sat down in his favorite chair with a balloon glass of brandy cradled in one hand. It had done him a world of good to see how happy the near newlyweds were. Perhaps Amanda had made the right choice in marrying Craig, after all. They seemed to bring out the best in each other and it was difficult now for Matt to acknowledge the nature of his original objections to their marriage.

"My volunteer work at the base day-care center turned into a paying job," she had told Matt as the three of them sat in the living room. "I work there half days, then spend the other half working at the library."

Craig had remained next to her on the couch the whole time they talked, his arm around her shoulders. It was plain to see how proud he was of her accomplishments. Matt wondered if Amanda had ever told him about her temporary doubts, when she had been ready to give it all up and come home. Seeing her happiness now, he was glad he'd had a hand in sending her back where she so obviously belonged.

The new responsibilities had increased her self-confidence and made her feel a real part of Craig's life at the base. And she was making friends there.

Craig also had changed. Amanda's love seemed to give him new assuredness, and the nervousness that used to set Matt's teeth on edge was all but gone. Matt and Craig had even found a few things to talk about during their dinner earlier at a popular Bellevue restaurant.

The only thing that would have made the evening more enjoyable for Matt would have been Willie sitting in the fourth chair at their table.

Amanda's curiosity had been obvious, but Matt had changed the subject each time she'd managed to work Willie's name into the conversation.

"Where shall we go for dinner tomorrow night?" he'd asked.

"Oh," Mandy said, glancing at Craig, "we made plans to spend the evening with friends. But we could go to lunch."

She named a restaurant noted for its lovely greenery, fine French cuisine and peaceful atmosphere.

"I have a pretty full day," Matt said regretfully.

"Oh, please," Amanda said. "Can't you rearrange your schedule? I've wanted to go there ever since I first heard about the place, and it would mean so much more if you were there with us. Our treat."

Matt couldn't withstand her pleading. "If it means that much to you, I'll have my secretary change things around," he said. "But we would have had more time at dinner."

Perhaps the break in the middle of the day would be good for him. It would be nice to get away from the office for a while, since his work didn't seem to give him the satisfaction it once had.

WILLIE AND AUNT VIOLET turned their car over to the parking valet and went up the steps to the building that looked more like a refurbished farmhouse than a successful restaurant.

"Wasn't it nice of Amanda and Craig to think of lunch here?" Violet asked, taking off her black jersey gloves with the rhinestone-studded lace cuffs. "It's such a pretty day and Amanda said they have some lovely outside tables."

Willie smoothed down the gray skirt she had put on for the wedding that morning with a matching jacket and plain white blouse, and wished she had taken the time to change. All she had been able to do was to pat down her curly hair and reapply her coral lip gloss before they'd had to leave for the drive to West Seattle.

As they went through the massive double doors, she glanced around. Most of the patrons she saw were very dressed up.

"Preston party," Aunt Violet said to the hostess.

"Oh, yes. I believe the rest of your group has already arrived," the impeccably groomed young woman replied. "Right this way."

Willie couldn't help but look around as the hostess led them through the charming dining room with its open-beamed ceiling. The tables were covered with linen cloths and the chair seats were upholstered in a variety of country prints. Greenery was everywhere and the muted sounds of conversation filled the room.

The hostess pushed open a door made of beveled glass in a peacock design and stepped onto a washed aggregate sidewalk. Ahead was a charming garden with tables set among the trees and flower beds. It reminded Willie of an old-fashioned flower garden.

She was so busy looking around she almost bumped into Violet when the hostess came to a stop.

"Here we are," the woman said, pulling two more chairs up to the round glass table set with straw place mats.

Willie smiled down at Amanda and Craig. The smile froze in place as she met the gaze of the third person seated with them.

Matt.

The expression of surprise on his face almost convinced her he'd known no more about this luncheon than she had. Almost.

He rose with Craig while Aunt Violet sat down and greeted the others.

"Is there a problem?" the hostess asked when Willie remained standing.

She glanced around. People at neighboring tables were beginning to look in her direction. There was no way she could protest this unexpected surprise without causing a scene, and she didn't want to do that to her young friends, no matter how misplaced their meddling was.

She took the chair the hostess was holding out for her and sat down next to Matt, looking everywhere but at him.

Finally she looked up. One glance was enough to assure her that he was as compelling as ever. Even the blur of exhaustion on his face, which she assumed had come from handling some tough case, only served to make him more appealing. His navy pin-striped suit, red tie and pale blue shirt only strengthened the image of a busy, successful professional.

Next to all that understated male elegance, Willie felt like a slightly wrinkled frump in her plain suit and blouse. Managing to give a general greeting without focusing on Matt again, she picked up her menu and hid behind it.

Despite her efforts to relax, the meal was a tense one. Amanda, Craig and Aunt Violet did their best to keep the conversational ball rolling through the salad course and entrée, but the minute any of them stopped talking, a strained silence fell over the table.

Their waiter, looking as if he worked in a French café, was dressed in the traditional outfit of black waistcoat over a white shirt, with a long white apron wrapped around his hips. "Dessert?" he asked finally, whisking away their luncheon plates and refilling their thick coffee mugs.

All five of them declined.

As soon as he went to get the check, Aunt Violet cleared her throat. "I think we'll leave the two of you to enjoy your coffee," she said, avoiding Willie's sharp stare. "Craig and Amanda will take me home."

Willie realized that her earlier suspicion was true. Violet was in on this, too. They had probably set the whole thing up while Willie had been performing that wedding in her parlor yesterday.

"I had your secretary clear your calendar for the afternoon," Amanda told Matt. "Willie's free, too, so we hope the two of you will take this opportunity to talk out whatever is keeping you apart."

Willie saw Matt half rise out of his chair, knuckles white. Her own face flooded with embarrassment.

"You shouldn't have done this!" she exclaimed to the three matchmakers, who were now standing.

"That's right," Matt said.

Willie was surprised he was backing her up, until she realized he didn't want to be there any more than she did.

She slid back her chair. "My afternoon is not free. I have a couple of halls to check out."

Amanda blocked her escape. Her eyes were pleading. "Willie, please don't run off. Matt's been miserable and I know you have, too."

"Just a damned minute," Matt protested gruffly.

Willie shot a glance at Violet, who had the grace to look down at her hands, sheathed in the ornate black gloves.

"I see that we've been thoroughly discussed. But no amount of talk can bring Matt and me back together. We're too different."

"That's right," Matt agreed again.

Willie ignored the urge to step on his foot.

"We're direct opposites," he continued. "I'm practical, logical and clear thinking. Willie here is full of romantic, impractical, foolish notions. She wants a white knight to carry her off to his castle in the clouds, which is where her brain is half the time, anyway."

Willie noticed that the surrounding diners were following his oration with much interest. She was too upset to care.

"You see how it is?" she asked, flinging a hand in his direction. "I may have been foolish enough to fall in love with him, but that doesn't mean I'm not allowed to come to my senses before it's too late."

When she saw the satisfaction on Amanda's face, she realized what she had just disclosed.

"I knew it!" Amanda exclaimed, squeezing Craig's hand. She turned to Matt. "Now tell Willie that you love her."

He remained silent, his face curiously blank.

Willie was utterly, thoroughly humiliated, not only by the fact that she had revealed her love for Matt to half the diners in the garden, but also by his telling silence when he had the opportunity to save her further embarrassment by declaring his feelings. An opportunity he was going to ignore, and for one simple reason. He didn't love her.

Strangling a sob, willing the tears not to come until she was alone, Willie turned toward the side gate that led out of the walled garden. "I'll see you later," she chocked out before she turned and fled.

MATT STOOD on the wide deck at the back of his house, drink in hand, watching the family of ducks that waddled across the rolling lawn on their way to the water, as he tried to interest himself in fixing something for dinner.

He remembered with painful clarity the expression on Willie's face when she'd realized what she had admitted at their ill-fated luncheon that afternoon. His own shock at her unexpected revelation had been enough to keep him silent, until it was too late to salvage the situation.

By the time he had collected the wits scattered by her announcement, she'd run from the restaurant as if the very hounds of hell were snapping at her heels. When Matt recovered and followed her out the gate, it was only to see her car pulling from the parking lot onto the main street. He had thought about calling her, only to stop before he had finished dialing her number. What would he say?

As he took another sip from his glass, Violet's parting words when he had returned to the trio of guilty conspirators echoed in his head: *"I'll be at bingo all evening and I worry about Willie being alone tonight. I know she doesn't have any plans."*

Subtle, he mused, about as subtle as the luncheon had been.

He had thought about Willie all afternoon, wondering what he should do. The way she had thrown back in his face the offer of a job in his practice still smarted. Jim and Ann had both asked him when she was coming on board, and he hadn't known what to tell them.

Much as he had tried to control his thoughts that afternoon, they had not stayed on the firm. Now he set the glass down and absently scratched his chin as other memories continued to crowd in. Memories of Willie at the house, her hair spread across his pillow like a flame, her creamy arms coaxing him to her as if he were no stronger than a moth transfixed by her fiery appeal.

The image of her pixie face and flashing eyes, the sound of her laughter as she cheerfully punctured his complacency, the special glow she had when she was conducting one of her weddings, all were enough to make him ache with loneliness.

He shifted uncomfortably. Lord, he missed her. On so many levels. He thumped his fist on the railing. Luckily there was something he could do about the situation.

Matt glanced at his watch as he went inside and took the stairs two at a time. After a quick shower he pulled on faded, comfortable jeans and a plaid cotton shirt. Perhaps he had come on too strong, surprising her with his offer and giving her no time to get used to the idea of working with him. But he had wasted enough time with indecisive brooding. What was needed here was action.

He descended the stairs as quickly as he had climbed them, grabbed his keys and almost didn't remember to lock the front door behind him. Why hadn't he thought of this approach before?

First he would overwhelm Willie in the one area where they had always been compatible, distracting her with kisses and disarming her with lovemaking. Then, when she was feeling more mellow toward him, he would convince her that his previous offer had been made in her best interest. Once she was back in his arms, where she belonged, he would begin dealing with the tough part, their feelings for each other and whatever the future might hold.

WILLIE LOOKED OUT the lace curtains to the twilight beyond. She was bored and restless, unable to settle. Perhaps she should have taken Violet up on the invitation to join her and Rudy at bingo, but Willie knew she didn't feel up to being nice to any man that evening.

Everyone has someone, she thought morosely, watching the traffic rush past on the busy arterial that ran in front of the chapel. Amanda had Craig; Aunt Violet had probably more than her quota of gentlemen friends; even the clerk at the grocery store had been sporting a new engagement ring when Willie had walked over for a quart of milk.

She sighed, debated making some tea but couldn't seem to find the energy to fill the kettle. Her supper had grown cold before she'd finally thrown it away. Now she wandered into the parlor, sniffed the spicy red and white carnations in their cut-glass vases and adjusted the doily on one overstuffed chair.

Maybe I'll get a cat, she thought, sitting down on the old davenport. And learn to knit. She could picture the new sign: Willie Webster's Weddings and Handmade Afgans.

A lone tear trickled down her cheek as she thought of herself in the years to come, a stooped old lady known throughout the north end of Seattle as "that kindly spinster."

After dashing the moisture from her eyes and shrugging off the self-pitying thoughts, she made a quick check of the television listings. The parade of summer reruns decided her that a bath and an early night were what she needed the most. Perhaps she would even sleep.

She had just let the water out of the tub, toweled off and used the blow-dryer on her hair while hanging her head upside down, when she heard the doorbell. Grabbing her old chenille robe and wrapping it securely around her, she tried to smooth down her wayward hair as she hurried toward the door.

She peeked out the curtained window, but whoever was on the porch stood too close for her to see. No strange cars were parked out front. Perhaps it was the clerk from the mini supermarket next door, bringing over some day-old doughnuts. She often did that before she left for the evening, and in exchange Aunt Violet told her fortune free.

Willie opened the door. "I'm afraid that Aunt Violet—" The rest of what she had been about to say stuck somewhere in her suddenly dry throat.

"Hello, Willie." Matt's voice was deep, his eyes narrowed and glued to hers, as he held out a huge mixed bouquet swathed in green tissue paper.

Her hand reached out automatically to take the flowers as she dealt with the shock of seeing him. "What are you doing here?" Her tone was defensive. "Where did you park?"

He answered the second question first. "I left the car around the corner. I wasn't sure you'd answer the door if you knew it was me."

She didn't comment, not sure herself.

"We have to talk." His strong jaw had a determined set to it.

Willie was painfully aware of her ratty bathrobe and the hair standing out from her head. And she wasn't wearing a speck of makeup, not even mascara to darken her eyelashes.

"Now isn't a good time," she said quickly.

Matt's mouth turned up in a compelling smile. "Expecting company?" he asked, eyeing her robe and bare feet.

"No," she said. "But I don't feel up to another scene with you."

"I'm not here to make a scene," he said, shoving his foot against the open door. His voice deepened. "Please, just give me a few minutes."

He must have seen her hesitation. Before Willie could protest he had pushed the door open and come in, shutting it behind him.

"I've missed you," he murmured as she looked up at him, too busy drinking in his dear, familiar features to protest his actions.

She noticed again the lines of fatigue around his mouth and eyes. Had his sleep been as restless as hers?

"I missed you, too," she confessed.

He took the bunch of flowers from her unresisting fingers and laid them on the table in the entry. Then his hands came up to cup her face, his touch gentle. The look he directed at her mouth was as potent as a kiss. Willie shivered with longing.

Then he lowered his head. "I love you, too," he said, before his lips met hers.

Joy burst in Willie's chest like exploding fireworks, a reaction to both his words and the feel of his mouth on hers. Eagerly her hands came up to hold him close, encouraging him to deepen the kiss.

Matt needed no second invitation. Any plans he had of maneuvering Willie went up in smoke as she boldly touched the tip of her tongue to his. With a growl of pure need, he swept her into his arms.

Willie's busy fingers had freed several buttons on his shirt before he reached the bedroom, setting her down on the homemade quilt.

Matt sent up a silent prayer of thanks for Violet's interest in bingo as he came down beside Willie, nuzzling the sweet warmth tucked between her neck and shoulder.

To Matt she smelled of soap and lavender and the happiness that surrounded him whenever he was with her.

"God, I missed you," he said fervently as her hands finished dealing with the buttons of his shirt and parted it, slipping inside to caress his fevered skin. He shuddered at her touch, the joy of holding her once again mingling with the ache to possess her. Rational thought and all its related questions were pushed aside and forgotten as he yanked loose the sash of her robe and unwrapped her like an early Christmas present.

Willie arched upward, her hands urging him closer as he bent to caress one pale breast, then the other, scraping the beaded tip with his tongue before he drew it between his lips and tugged gently.

Willie's gasp of pleasure drove him higher, even as his questing fingers skimmed downward, past the downy skin of her stomach to the tight curls beyond. He was barely conscious that Willie was doing her best to rid him of his shirt until she pulled impatiently, coming half off the bed. Distracted, Matt took a moment to peel away his remaining clothing. Then he returned to her, his mouth searing hers as his hand took up its earlier quest.

Willie gasped again as he skimmed over her. His fingers ran back up the sensitive skin of her inner thigh, and she opened to him without further urging.

Matt lowered his head, teasing her knee with his tongue, nibbling gently as she thrashed back and forth, her nails gripping the skin drawn tight across his shoulders.

When neither of them could stand it a second longer, he worked his way to the very center of her desire, bestowing the most intimate of kisses.

Beneath him, Willie arched upward, sensation exploding through her. She dug her fingers into his hair, holding him close as he continued to caress her wildly sensitive flesh. As soon as her response had waned to a series of quivering aftershocks, Matt raised himself up and buried his face against her breasts, at the same time sliding into her.

Willie wrapped herself around him as he thrust deeply, anchoring his big body close. As she felt her response gathering again, the tiny spasms building to a shattering peak, Matt plunged even deeper, holding her tight against him. He groaned her name. Together they tumbled into oblivion.

Matt's breathing had finally smoothed out, when he shifted his weight, moving onto his back and cradling Willie next to him. She was stroking his muscular, hairy calf with her toes, running them up and down, as he linked his fingers through hers, his breath on her cheek. Finally she could stand his stare no longer. She turned, looking into his dark eyes.

"Did you mean what you said before?" she couldn't prevent herself from asking.

Matt understood instantly. "Yes," he murmured, voice husky. "I love you, Willie."

She curled closer, happiness sizzling through her. All the pain and loneliness she had suffered were forgotten in the path of his words. To Willie, love meant commitment and commitment meant marriage. Without thinking, she spoke her heart.

"I have some terrific ideas for a ceremony," she said dreamily, sifting her fingers through his black chest hair. "Something really romantic. Do you think that Amanda would stand up for me?"

Beside her, Matt stiffened. As she raised up and looked at his face again she saw that his open expression of love had retreated behind an emotionless mask. Once again she had spoken without thinking.

"What are you talking about?" he asked, sitting up.

Willie was confused, hurt, embarrassed.

"I, uh, nothing. I was just rambling," she said, pulling the sheet up to hide her nakedness. How could she have leaped to such hasty conclusions? She hadn't even waited for Matt to propose before she'd started talking weddings to him. Her cheeks burned as she reached for her robe, holding the sheet up in front of her.

"Wait a minute," Matt said, wrapping a hand around her wrist.

Willie stopped, and forced herself to look at him. He was frowning as his dark eyes bored into hers.

"I know we need to talk," he said. He raked his free hand through his hair, leaving it sticking up in untidy spikes.

Willie waited quietly for him to continue, her insides tap dancing with nervousness.

Matt let out a gusty sigh. "Dammit, Willie, I'm just not ready to discuss my feelings."

Willie wouldn't have thought it possible to be more embarrassed than she already was, but his words made her feel as if she had been pressuring an unwilling victim. Tears of humiliation backed up behind her eyelids.

"I understand," she managed to say, looking away as he released her.

As she scrambled for her robe, Matt moved toward the opposite edge of the bed. His feet hit the floor and he reached for his scattered clothes. All he had been thinking of was holding Willie again, loving her. He needed time to work out the rest. Old fears, new challenges and suffocating panic all combined within him to propel his movements as he drew on his shorts and jeans. He had to be alone.

When he looked over his shoulder, Willie was already standing, her old robe covering her with the modesty of a nun. Her eyes were wide with pain and disappointment.

Matt hesitated, knowing he should say something to erase the awkwardness that had sprung between them. He loved Willie. But he had to sort things out, and he had to do it alone. Thinking straight was more than he could manage when she was near, seducing him with her scent, her touch, the laughter that made him feel so alive, so lighthearted. Matt wasn't sure if he even trusted his own judgment anymore when it came to her, and it was that fear that sealed his lips as he finished dressing.

"Matt?" Her voice was soft, tentative.

He slipped on his shoes and looked at her. Her face was open, trusting, despite her discomfort. He had an idea what it cost her.

He dropped a kiss on her lips. The unspoken words between them were a living presence. Matt didn't think he could go on without her, but past hurts stilled his tongue. The light faded from Willie's eyes as he remained silent. She turned away.

"Aunt Violet will be coming home soon," she said, voice divested of color.

Matt put a hand on her shoulder, willing her to understand. "I'll call you," he said. The words sounded hollow even to him.

She didn't turn around. After a pause he left the room, trying to rid himself of that last picture of her, turned away, shoulders not quite square.

He was only halfway home, when he realized what a fool he had been. Willie loved him and he loved her. That was no more of a guarantee than anyone had, but as soon as Matt listened to his heart instead of his insecurity he knew that love was enough. Willie was worth any risk, any chance he had to take. What they had together was strong enough to withstand any challenge.

Gripping the wheel, he was about to turn around and head back to her house, when he glanced at his watch. Aunt Violet would most certainly be home. They might both be sleeping.

He had waited this many years to find happiness and the courage to grab it. He could wait a few more hours. He would call Willie in the morning, see her, tell her what was in his heart.

When he did finally call, waiting impatiently until he was sure they would both be up, Violet answered the phone.

Her voice, after she identified herself, was surprisingly cool and formal.

"Willie's already left for the day," she told him.

"Where will she be? When is she expected home?" Matt could hardly contain his impatience. He should have gone back last night. This waiting was driving him crazy.

"I can't tell you where she is," Violet responded. "She doesn't want to talk to you or to see you. Matthew Bailey, what have you done to that poor girl now?"

"I'M NOT HERE," Willie said, shaking her head adamantly.

Aunt Violet took back the telephone receiver she had been holding out. "I'm sorry, Matt," she said. "Willie can't come to the phone."

Willie waited until Violet had finished saying goodbye and hung up before she spoke again. "There's no point in trying to get me to talk to him. Matt was right in the first place." Her eyes filled with tears and she turned away so Violet wouldn't see. "Love is a fairy tale," she said. "Wishful thinking."

"Bullfeathers!" Violet rattled the clean dishes from the drainer as she put them away. "You've performed enough weddings to know that just isn't true."

Willie was getting tired of defending her position. She just wanted to be able to forget the whole thing.

Amanda had called several times, she and Craig had come over once and Matt had called every day for the past week, as well as sending flowers. She would have thought he'd get the message by now. She didn't want to see him. Ever again.

"I'll be in the garden," she said, grabbing a worn pair of gloves and slipping outside. The weather was changing; soon it would be time to rake dead leaves and clean out the flower beds. She had always liked the fall before, but now it depressed her, as did almost everything else.

Wearing the gloves and wielding pruning shears like a crusader's sword, she began to cut back a forsythia that was crowding out the surrounding bushes. *I wish everyone would leave me alone*, she told herself as she hacked away the leafy branches.

Matt was bound to get tired of calling her any day now. Then her life could get back to normal. Somewhere down the line she would regain her enthusiasm for the weddings that used to delight her. She would forget that half of them were doomed to fail and only see the happiness radiated in the newlyweds' faces.

Willie began to whistle tunelessly as she turned her attention to a pink dogwood with dead branches. "When one door closes, another opens," her father used to say. She could hardly wait for that new door. She was doing her best to slam the old one shut, but it was still painful.

SEATED in his spacious, lonely living room, Matt resisted the urge to slam down the receiver after yet another unsuccessful attempt to make contact with Willie. He was beginning to feel he knew her aunt better than he did Willie herself; he had talked to the older woman often enough in the past few days.

Willie had gone so far as to install an answering machine on her phone. If Violet wasn't home he got the recording. Each time he'd sat through the strains of the wedding march before the beep, he couldn't help but wonder if Willie had done it deliberately.

"No luck?" Amanda asked, coming into the room with two tall glasses of iced tea. She set one down by his chair and took the other with her to the leather couch.

"No. I think she was there, but she wouldn't come to the phone." Matt sighed, drumming his fingers on the arm of the chair. What if Willie was serious and they really were through? He couldn't stand the idea of never holding her again, never seeing her eyes twinkle as she said something outrageous, never feeling his heart lift at her faith in people's basic goodness.

"I'm running out of ideas," he told his sister, who had taken a long weekend off work to visit him while Craig's ship was out on more sea trials. "You got any?"

Amanda thought for a moment, sipping her tea. "Well," she said, "I always pictured you as a man of action. You've called. You've sent flowers. Nothing has worked. Maybe it's time to go see her face-to-face, force your way in if you have to and demand that she listen. When you and I had a problem you never sat around waiting for an invitation." She grinned.

Matt's answering smile was edged with regret. "I thought you knew Willie's temper better than that. She'd have me in an arm lock and out the door before I could ask her how she is." He hadn't forgotten the view of her ceiling he'd had from the Oriental carpet.

"It's not like you to sound so defeated, big brother. What's happened to that Bailey stubborn streak you always tell me we both inherited?"

Matt shrugged. "Maybe it's destiny," he said. "Maybe it just wasn't meant to be." He sighed despondently and swirled the ice cubes in his glass.

Amanda leaped up, slapping her hands on her narrow hips. "Am I hearing you right?" she demanded. "Matthew Bailey rolling over like a friendly hound dog who wants his stomach scratched? I don't believe this. Where's the guy who passed the bar in the top ten percent first time out? Who opened his own firm and made it a success in less than a year? Who has stood up to every good lawyer in the county and whipped most?"

Matt couldn't help but shake his head with admiration as her voice rose steadily. Amanda had come into her own these months since her marriage.

When he remained silent she began again. "You've surmounted bigger obstacles than one little redhead." She paused to take a deep breath, maybe to give him time to answer. When he didn't she asked, "Don't you love her anymore?" Amanda's stare was accusing.

"Of course I love her!" Matt said without thinking. "You don't just turn that off."

Amanda's expression turned smug, but he ignored it.

"Willie and I have always been at cross-purposes," he continued. "I used to think she had her head permanently stuck in some romantic pink cloud. Now as soon as *I* realize I can't live without her, *she* apparently decides that love is a myth, after all. I'm *not* giving up, but I'm sure stumped."

"You'll think of something," Amanda said encouragingly. "I don't know how she could resist you for long."

"Thanks," Matt said absently, but he was thinking about something else. Something Willie had said. He mulled it over carefully, while Amanda fidgeted, unable to contain her impatience.

"Matt? What is it?"

It was his turn to come to his feet. "Hell, no," he said. "I'm not ready to give up. I've been going about this all wrong. Good ol' predictable Matt taking the logical path. Well, no more Mr. Nice Guy. It's time I beat Willie at her own game, and maybe I've come up with the way to do just that."

Amanda plopped back down and picked up her glass of iced tea. "Tell me," she said. "What's your plan?"

Matt began to pace back and forth. "Yes," he said, half to himself. "It's so crazy it just might work." Leaving Amanda to stew with curiosity, he left the room, mumbling to himself.

"ARE YOU SURE you have everything you need?" Aunt Violet asked for the third time.

Willie searched her briefcase. "I think so," she said. "I don't know why I'm so nervous."

"You've performed weddings for the cream of society before," Violet said, wiping a fingerprint off the black leather case with her hankie. "Don't worry about this one. You'll do fine."

Willie didn't bother trying to explain it was Matt's continued silence that was making her jumpy and unhappy. The phone calls and flowers had stopped abruptly a week before. So why couldn't she accept the fact that he had given up? That was what she wanted. Wasn't it?

"It was so nice of Judge Armstrong to think of me," she said, trying hard to concentrate as she looked into the full-length mirror on her bedroom wall, licking her finger and smoothing it over one eyebrow. "He could have gotten anyone in Seattle to fill in for him."

"And he gave you a week's notice. I'm glad you could shift your schedule around. Who knows what this ceremony will lead to in the way of other contacts?"

Willie had twisted around to check the backs of her nylons for snags. "I met the judge only once. I'm surprised he remembered me. Too bad his wife had to have surgery this week, though. I hope she recovers quickly."

"I'm sure she will," Violet said, getting Willie's caftan out of the closet. "Are you positive you want this one?" She held up the rainbow striped garment so that its fine pleats shimmered in the soft light.

Willie nodded, fluffing out her hair. "When I described it to the bride she thought it would look terrific with her attendants' dresses. She has a dozen bridesmaids and they're all wearing different pastel colors." Willie eyed the caftan thoughtfully. "It's one of my favorites, too. Much more cheerful than the navy, don't you think?"

Before Violet could answer, Willie inserted large, thin gold hoops into her ears and slipped several matching bangles onto one wrist. Her flat-heeled shoes were gold kid.

"The bride's short," she said to Violet, who was putting the caftan into the garment bag lying across the bed. "She asked me not to wear heels, and I guess none of her bridesmaids will, either."

Finally Willie was ready. She had taken pains with her hair and makeup—pleased with the results—and had dabbed her favorite scent on every pulse point she could think of. "Wish me luck," she said, tilting her cheek for her aunt's kiss. "I'll see you later."

"You'll be a hit," Violet said, following her to the door. "They can't help but love you."

"The bride and groom will be too busy gawking at each other even to know I'm there," Willie said. "Until I pronounce them husband and wife, anyway."

AN HOUR LATER, Willie was congratulating herself on how well the ceremony was going. Twin ring bearers, nephews of the bride, had come down the aisle without incident, followed by two little flower girls in long dresses and patent leather shoes.

The younger one, who looked about three, carried her basket of rose petals proudly until her sister whispered in her ear, obviously reminding her to toss the petals. With a studious expression, the little girl stopped dead in the middle of the aisle, dumped the whole basket of petals on the white runner and moved on with a satisfied smile as the onlookers chuckled softly.

When the flower girls got to the front of the hall, Willie gave them a wink before they turned to the side. The older one winked back and the younger squeezed both eyes shut tight, flashing matching dimples.

As Willie stood facing the audience, waiting for the parade of attendants to finish, the image of a dark-haired man flashed into her mind's eye. Her smile faltered for just a moment as she banished him sternly, concentrating on the first jubilant strains of the wedding march.

The bride came down the aisle, escorted by her white-haired father, a pillar of the community, as the groom waited nervously, shifting his weight from one foot to the other. As soon as the bride stopped beside him, he became calm and faced Willie proudly. Smiling at both of them, she began speaking.

They had just finished reciting their vows and the groom was kissing his brand-new bride, when the side door by Willie slammed open, hitting the wall with a bang.

She didn't turn her head to see what the interruption was until the bride pulled out of her husband's embrace and pointed a finger, eyes wide. When some of the guests began talking—a babble of confused voices—Willie finally shifted her gaze to the source of the untimely intrusion.

What she saw almost caused her to drop the white prayer book she held to her heart. Indeed the sight almost caused her heart itself to stop.

A pirate was standing in the doorway.

Willie knew he was a pirate because he wore a black patch over one eye, a red rose in his teeth and a long silver saber at his waist. She blinked, wondering if skipping lunch was causing her to hallucinate.

The pirate was still there, dressed in a dashing white shirt, tight black pants and leather boots that reached almost to his knees. Willie stared harder. Despite the dark stubble on his chin and the eye patch, he looked startlingly familiar.

Beside her, the groom turned back to where the bride remained motionless. "I thought you told me you broke it off with Chandler," he said accusingly.

Before his intended could answer, the pirate whipped the rose from his teeth and laughed loudly, a diabolical sound. He strode boldly forward, saber clinking at his side.

"Fear not," he said. "'Tis not the bride I come for."

Willie barely resisted a hysterical giggle at the sound of the familiar voice. Before she could think of a thing to say, the pirate had approached her, stepping around the stupefied groom and his dumbstruck bride.

With a sweeping bow, the pirate offered Willie the rose. She didn't know if she should laugh or be furious as she stared up into his flashing brown eyes. Behind him, the murmurs were getting louder.

"What do you think you're doing?" she whispered, hardly able to believe that Matthew Bailey, attorney at law, would create such a spectacle.

"Pay attention," he whispered back, "and perhaps you'll figure it out." With another dashing smile, he turned to face the rest of the room, bowing again.

The bride, who was clutching her husband's arm, looked ready to faint, and the groom's face had turned a dusky shade of red.

"I beg your indulgence," Matt said in his best court-room voice. "I come not for the bride. 'Tis the justice of the peace who has taken my fancy. And stolen my black heart in the process."

A gasp went up from the crowd, followed by a further buzz of voices. A laugh rang out.

"Go for it!" someone shouted.

Willie's hand covered her mouth, which had dropped open in astonishment. When Matt turned to her, she backed away from his outstretched arm.

"I'm conducting a wedding," she exclaimed, trying to hold on to at least a shred of dignity. "I can't possibly leave now!"

"On the contrary," Matt said, loud enough for everyone to hear. "They're legally bound. Your work here is finished." He lowered his voice. "Wouldn't have been polite of me to leave them hanging, would it now?" he asked her quietly.

"Just what do you expect me to do?" Willie crossed her arms over her chest.

With another bold grin, Matt stepped forward and snatched her into his arms.

"Put me down!" she shouted, beating at him with her free hand. In the other she still held the rose he had given her, and her prayer book. She noticed how broad and powerful his chest looked beneath the deeply veed pirate shirt, and had to resist the urge to smooth her palm over his warm skin.

Matt whirled around, holding Willie cradled against his heart in a steely embrace.

"Sorry for the interruption, folks," he said. "Congratulations," he added over his shoulder to the bride and groom as he began to carry Willie from the room.

The bride, who had recovered from her shock when Matt had said he hadn't come for her, shouted, "Kiss her!"

"An excellent idea," Matt replied, pausing. "My pleasure, madam."

"Lay one lip on me and you're dead meat," Willie ground out between her teeth. She would never live this down!

"I laugh in the face of danger," Matt told her before he bent his head.

The kiss he bestowed on her was neither brief nor restrained. His lips molded themselves hotly to hers as his arms gripped her tighter. His tongue sought entry boldly, until Willie's head began to spin and her mouth opened willingly to receive him. When his tongue tangled with hers she almost forgot where they were. She'd hungered for his kisses since she and Matt had parted in anger. Common sense melted in the heat of passion as she returned the enthusiastic salute, absorbing his taste and touch with darting strokes.

A burst of applause broke the spell and brought Willie partway back to earth. She was still slightly dazed when Matt tossed off a jaunty wave and began to carry her from the hall, amid applause, cheers and whistles of encouragement.

This was certainly a wedding no one in the room would ever forget.

The last thing she saw before the best man shut the door was the bride and groom in a passionate embrace as organ music burst forth.

"Where are you taking me?" she demanded as Matt continued to carry her down the granite-floored hallway of the venerable old club. Luckily the immediate area appeared to be temporarily deserted.

"Somewhere private," Matt said, not looking at her. His cheeks were pink beneath the faint growth of beard.

For the first time Willie began to realize what the scene in the room behind them must have cost him. Matt was a proud man, used to acting in a correct and dignified manner. For him to do what he had just done was almost inconceivable. Willie's arms tightened around his neck and she decided to relax and find out what else he had planned.

"Well, it's your show," she said with a grin when he glanced down at her.

Matt's eyebrows climbed in astonishment. He'd thought she would be furious, that he'd have to do all he could to calm her down. Instead she was smiling up at him, her eyes flooded with green and gold shimmers, as if he had just done something wonderful. She was certainly consistent in her ability to astound him.

As he carried her toward the small, private room Judge Armstrong had assured him would be unlocked and waiting, the sword bounced against his leg, almost tripping him. Matt stumbled, cursing under his breath, and his grip tightened on Willie, who clung harder to his neck. Her scent rose around him, and his body responded in an uncomfortably predictable manner.

This had better work. There was no Plan B.

At last Matt spied the room he sought. Shifting her weight, he turned the knob and kicked open the door. He thought he heard Willie mutter, "My hero," but couldn't be certain as he flicked on the light switch. In the small sitting room was a couch, two chairs and a table, on which rested a bottle of champagne in ice and two fluted glasses, just as Matt had requested.

"What a nice touch," Willie murmured, looking around.

"Thanks," Matt said as he shut the door behind them and released her slowly.

Willie slid down his body until her feet touched the floor. Since she was wearing flat-heeled shoes, he seemed even bigger than he normally did, looming over her like the rogue he impersonated. With a shiver of anticipation, she reached up and gently removed the eye patch, working its elasticized cord over the bandanna tied around his head. In one ear winked a gold earring.

"You've thought of everything," she said, staring up at him.

There was a fierce expression on his face as he returned her stare with an intense one of his own. "I had to," he replied. "It's important, the most important thing I've ever done."

His intensity frightened her. "What do you mean?"

"First things first," Matt said more calmly. He took her hands in his, raising them and kissing the backs, one after the other. His warm breath on her knuckles made Willie shiver with reaction. All in all, it was turning into a very strange afternoon.

His eyes had darkened to black and his features were taut with something she couldn't identify. His shoulders under her hands were tense, the muscles rigid.

A wave of longing threatened to make her cry. A dozen questions crowded the tip of her tongue and hope, like a bright, pure flame, started to blaze inside her.

When Matt came closer, she tipped back her head to meet his descending mouth. The kiss they exchanged was achingly sweet, gentle as a feather, and filled with a pure promise that did bring the moisture to her eyes. Wordlessly they drew apart, her gaze riveted to his face.

His expression was almost haunted as he drew her to the couch and lightly pushed her down. He took her hand in his again, and now he towered above her.

"I have something to say." He cleared his throat and she could see a swallow ripple down the strong column of his neck.

Willie's eyes widened. If she didn't know Matt to be the confident, arrogant man he was, she would have sworn he was nervous. She smiled encouragingly, wishing he would continue and ease the curiosity that was eating her up.

Matt sighed and dropped down beside her on the couch. "I've been a jerk," he began, surprising her.

Willie opened her mouth to protest, but he shook his head. "I have," he said. "You attracted me because you were so bright and lively, like a butterfly. Then I set about to change everything I had admired in the first place."

With a shock Willie realized she had been trying to do exactly the same thing. The assuredness, the quiet confidence, the rock solid stability and logic that made him what he was had been the very things she had come to resent. With an effort she remained silent, waiting for him to continue.

"You know about my parents' marriage," he said, shifting on the couch. "It wasn't happy and I used to wish they would separate. Instead they were killed." He paused for a moment. "I guess I felt guilty. Then I married Michelle, thinking we would be a family for Amanda. That didn't work out, either."

Willie smiled encouragingly, hanging on every word.

"All that, along with my job, convinced me that love and marriage were just so much propaganda. Somewhere along the line I lost faith in my own ability to make a commitment, to sustain that kind of relationship. I told myself I didn't believe in love, but what I was really doing was denying the very thing I wanted—no, *needed*—above everything else." He took a deep breath, his dark eyes searching hers.

"You don't have to—" Willie began, but again Matt shook his head.

"I do have to," he said quietly. "You brought color to my life, and music and joy. I wanted you so much it scared the hell out of me. So I set about to change you into someone who wouldn't, couldn't, reach me." He frowned. "Am I making any sense?"

Willie ran one hand down his tense jaw, her fingers stroking his cheek. The whiskers rasped against her skin. "You're making all kinds of sense," she said. "So much that I understand my own actions better. You aren't the only one who was afraid."

Matt sighed deeply, as if a great weight had been lifted. He gathered her close. "I love you," he murmured into her hair. "I love everything about you and I wouldn't—" she felt his smile "—change a hair on your head." She felt his hand sift through her curls, pushing them away from her face.

Willie's eyes fluttered shut, enjoying the caress. Then the cushion next to her shifted and her eyes flew back open. Matt had slid to the floor next to her, down onto one knee.

"I don't plan on ever doing this again," he said, smiling tenderly, though his face bore the marks of considerable strain. "So I might as well do it right."

He took her hand in his and stared deep into her eyes. "Willie, will you marry me and make me the happiest man on earth?"

It took a moment for the words Willie had, in the darkness and privacy of her own bedroom, imagined him speaking to actually sink in. When they did she gasped, clutching the front of his silky pirate shirt.

"Did you just propose?" she squeaked, still unable to believe that what she had longed for with all her heart was really happening.

His smile deepened. "Yes, I did. But I haven't gotten an answer yet."

Willie threw her arms around his neck, launching herself at him with such enthusiasm that he swayed before he righted himself. His hands clasped her waist as she buried her face in his neck.

"Yes!" she sang out. "You can bet your saber I'll marry you." She was laughing and crying all at once, finally convinced that Matt was sincere, sane and dead serious despite the way he was dressed. What he had done assured her that they could surmount any obstacle that might come up.

When she kissed him, she touched her hand to his cheek. To her surprise, she felt moisture there. When the kiss ended she opened her eyes to see that his eyes were wet, their dark lashes damp and spiky. Her heart melted with love.

Matt reached his hand into his pocket and pulled out a small box. When he opened it, Willie sucked in her breath.

"I thought you might like something different," he said, voice husky. He took Willie's hand and slid the ring onto her finger. It fit perfectly.

"Do you like it?" he asked anxiously.

"I love it!"

The ring was gold, with an oval-cut diamond surrounded by a border of carved green jade and smaller diamonds.

"Thank you," Willie said, pulling him close for another kiss. "It's perfect."

"You aren't just saying that? We could—"

"I *love* it," she said firmly.

"Good." Relief softened his features. "Now tell me some of those ideas you had for a perfect ceremony," he said. "I'm ready to hear them."

Willie glanced past him at the champagne. "I'd feel more comfortable if you got up off your knees."

He turned his head, following her gaze. "I almost forgot." He rose, pulling her with him, and walked over to the small table. Opening the bottle, he filled the two glasses and handed her one.

"To us," he said, curving his free arm around her waist.

They each took a sip, then kissed again. Several moments passed in a golden haze before Willie remembered his previous question.

"I guess that free-falling from a plane is out," she said with a straight face, "as is any ceremony conducted underwater." She shuddered at the idea, then thought a moment, trying to recall the most unusual weddings she had performed or heard about.

"We could get married on the top of a mountain, or the Space Needle, or on board a ferry."

Matt bent toward her, stopping the flow of words with another kiss. "What's wrong with a nice, traditional wedding?" he asked. "In a church, with bridesmaids. You in white with a veil. Me in a tux. Aunt Violet with her hair tinted to color-coordinate with the attendants' dresses." His smile widened. "A three-tiered cake, maybe an ice sculpture in the shape of something unabashedly romantic like a pair of doves. All our friends around." His expression grew sober. "Would that be so dull?" he asked.

Willie's eyes flooded with fresh tears at the picture he had painted. "I thought you would want something modern and innovative," she said. "Trendy."

Matt shook his head slowly. "I want you, any way I can get you. It's my last wedding. Yours, too, as a bride. Let's make some memories," he whispered against her mouth.

Again he kissed her, and she could taste the champagne on his mouth. This kiss was filled with promise and commitment.

When they broke apart, Matt glanced at his watch. "Let's get out of here," he said.

Willie agreed wholeheartedly. "I like both those ideas." She glanced around the small room, assuming that Matt had a change of clothes here.

"Hell, no," he exclaimed when she asked him. "I don't embarrass you, do I? Personally I kind of like the new me."

With another shout of laughter, he scooped her back into his arms and flung open the door. Several people in the hallway stopped to stare as he carried her toward the imposing main entrance.

As they emerged from the building, pausing at the top of the flight of stone steps, a roving photographer quickly knelt before them, snapping the shutter of his camera. He had gotten an anonymous tip that hanging around the building might get him a story.

The last thing he had expected to see was the very successful, dignified and locally well-known attorney, Matthew Bailey, dressed as a pirate and carrying a gorgeous redhead down the steps of the staid old club, her hair an orange halo and her rainbow striped caftan billowing around them as his saber clinked at his side.

"Mr. Bailey," the photographer shouted, scrambling after them, "could I ask you a few questions?"

Matt looked at the woman in his arms and they both laughed. "Not today," he said, as she beamed at him with pride. "We've got a wedding to go to. Besides, you probably wouldn't believe me, anyway."

MATTHEW BAILEY and Wilhelmina Webster were married in a small white chapel with sunlight streaming through the stained-glass windows. Amanda and Craig Preston were the matron of honor and best man; Violet Dibble, her hair tinted a becoming shade of silver and studded with artificial butterflies, gave the bride away. The chapel was filled with the beaming couple's friends.

At the reception that followed, Willie hitched up her satin skirts to reveal a black eye patch strapped above her knee instead of the traditional blue garter. After she tossed it into the crowd she was heard to say that this was by far the most perfect wedding she had ever attended.

ANNOUNCING . . .

Harlequin
Romance
#3000

The Lost Moon Flower
by Bethany Campbell

**Look for it this August
wherever Harlequins are sold**

HR 3000-1

HARLEQUIN Temptation

COMING NEXT MONTH

Your favorite stories with a brand-new look!!

HARLEQUIN

American Romance

Beginning next month, the four American Romance titles will feature a new, contemporary and sophisticated cover design. As always, each story will be a terrific romance with mature characters and a realistic plot that is uniquely North American in flavor and appeal.

Watch your bookshelves for a **bold** look!

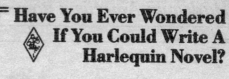

Have You Ever Wondered If You Could Write A Harlequin Novel?

Here's great news—Harlequin is offering a series of cassette tapes to help you do just that. Written by Harlequin editors, these tapes give practical advice on how to make your characters—and your story—come alive. There's a tape for each contemporary romance series Harlequin publishes.

Mail order only

All sales final
